DISNEY

AGENT STITCH

A STUDY IN SLIME

For James and Emma—the best of experiments
—S.B.

Published by Disney Press, an imprint of Buena Vista Books, Inc. No part of this book may be reproduced or transmitted in any form or by any means, electronic or mechanical, including photocopying, recording, or by any information storage and retrieval system, without written permission from the publisher. For information address Disney Press, 1200 Grand Central Avenue, Glendale, California 91201.

First Hardcover Edition, June 2022
1 3 5 7 9 10 8 6 4 2
FAC-034274-22112
ISBN 978-1-368-06710-2
Printed in the United States of America
Library of Congress Control Number: 2021946498
Visit disneybooks.com

DISNEP
AGENT
STITCH
A STUDY IN SLIME

Written by **STEVE BEHLING**

Illustrated by **ARIANNA REA**

DISNEP PRESS

Los Angeles • New York

CLASSIFIED FILE

GALACTIC DETECTIVE AGENCY

Full Name: Stitch

Aliases: Experiment 626

Distinguishing Features: Four arms, two of which can be retracted into subject's body; retractable antennae; back spines

Planet of Origin: Unknown (Dr. Jumba Jookiba has yet to reveal full details of creature's origin)

CLASSIFIED

Present Location: E-arth

Occupation: Abomination, dog

Known Associates: Lilo Pelekai, Nani Pelekai, Dr. Jumba Jookiba, Pleakley

Background: Created by Dr. Jumba Jookiba, Experiment 626 was initially captured by the Galactic Federation and exiled to a deserted asteroid. Subject escaped custody and traveled to the planet E-arth. Subject joined forces with E-arthers Lilo Pelekai and her sister, Nani, successfully avoiding attempts of Galactic Federation representatives Jookiba and Agent Pleakley to recapture him. Subject also escaped capture by Captain Gantu. Subject now lives on E-arth as part of the Pelekai family, under the protection of the Grand Councilwoman.

CLASSIFIED FILE

GALACTIC DETECTIVE AGENCY

Full Name: Pelekai, Lilo

Aliases: None known

Distinguishing Features: Incredible cuteness disguises great bravery, inner strength.

Planet of Origin: E-arth

Present Location: E-arth

Occupation: Human child

Known Associates: Nani Pelekai (sister), Stitch, Dr. Jumba Jookiba, Pleakley, Scrump*

Background: Lilo Pelekai is a young girl who was born and raised on the planet E-arth and lives with her sister (Nani). Subject first encountered Experiment 626, aka Stitch, in what E-arthers call an animal shelter. According to subject, 626 disguised himself as a "dog," which is apparently some kind of pet. Subject displays similar temperament as 626, such as quick temper, impulsive attitude, and general disregard for the rules. However, it should be noted that subject possesses an inner goodness and a desire to make the world a better place. The Grand Councilwoman suggests subject has influenced 626 for the better.

* NOTE: Need to investigate this "Scrump." They look suspicious.

CLASSIFIED FILE

GALACTIC DETECTIVE AGENCY

Full Name: Jookiba, Dr. Jumba

Aliases: Unknown

Distinguishing Features: Four eyes

Planet of Origin: Quelte Quan

Present Location: E-arth

Occupation: Scientist, mad

CLASSIFIED

Known Associates: Pleakley, Stitch, Lilo Pelekai, Nani Pelekai, Experiments 1–625

Background: Dr. Jumba Jookiba (degree obtained from Evil Genius University) conducted a series of unauthorized, highly illegal experiments involving the creation of creatures. Subject dubbed these creatures "Experiments" and gave each a number, starting with 1. His 626th Experiment, aka Stitch, was the absolute worst. Subject was apprehended by the Galactic Federation and eventually sent to E-arth to retrieve Experiment 626, who went into hiding. Subject failed at this mission but earned a reprieve from the Galactic Federation; now lives with the Pelekai family.

CLASSIFIED FILE

GALACTIC DETECTIVE AGENCY

Full Name: Pleakley, Wendy

Aliases: Agent Pleakley (former)

Distinguishing Features: One eye, three legs

Planet of Origin: Plorgonar

Present Location: E-arth

Occupation: Former agent of the Galactic Federation; mosquito expert

Known Associates: Dr. Jumba Jookiba, Stitch, Lilo Pelekai, Nani Pelekai, wig

Background: Former agent Pleakley spent a good deal of his career working for the Galactic Federation. Chiefly known as an expert on a species of insects called mosquitoes, from the planet E-arth, subject fell out of favor when he and Dr. Jumba Jookiba failed to apprehend Experiment 626. Currently residing on E-arth with the Pelekai family, subject continues to prove somewhat helpful to the Galactic Federation, and by "somewhat helpful," we mean "not entirely helpful."

SCHLORP!

It was midnight in Paris, France. Many people were at home, tucked into their beds, probably snoring really loud, which is super annoying for people who have to hear them. Still others were hanging out in the city, enjoying a nice, peaceful spring evening.

Well, except for the guy who was running down the alley. He looked very, *very* afraid—which was unusual, because this was a big burly guy who appeared like nothing could frighten him. As he sprinted along, he knocked a garbage can down behind him. Then another, and another. They hit the pavement with a loud symphony of metallic clangs. The man hoped that the garbage cans might slow *it* down.

He glanced over his shoulder and saw a strange green glow fill the dark alley.

The thing that had been chasing him was coming closer . . . closer . . . and closer.

"Whatever you are," the man said, "you picked the wrong guy to mess with."

The glowing green thing didn't answer as it crept closer, moving slowly, as if it had all the time in the world. As it inched closer, there was a loud noise.

"This isn't my first rodeo," the man said, then turned around and immediately ran face-first into a chain-link fence. Looking up, he could see that the fence was ten, maybe twelve, feet high. He had no choice but to climb.

The man jumped, and the metal rattled as he hoisted himself up.

Whatever the glowing green thing was, it continued to slink along the alleyway, its pace quickening.

SCHLORP . . . SCHLORP . . .

SCHLORP!!!

The man was almost at the top of the fence when his right hand slipped, and he fell to the ground, landing on a pile of garbage bags. He got to his feet and turned around.

The thing that had been chasing him was the last thing the man would see, and it looked just . . .

like . . .

THIS!

WHOA!

HANG ON JUST A MINUTE!

Do you REALLY want to know what happened
to that guy, and what that glowing green
thing was that we're not allowed to see?

☐ YES ☐ NO (but really, yes)

(check one)

And what does this have to do with Stitch?

☐ I was kind of hoping the book
would tell me that.

If you checked any of these boxes,
and even if you didn't, turn the page
and you will discover an unbelievable
mystery we like to call . . .

~~Stitch's Super-Fun Spring Adventure!~~

A Study in Slime!

(Much better title for a mystery book)

CHAPTER 1

CONFIDENTIAL

FIELD TRIP

CONFIDENTIAL

Stitch rested his chin in his paw, tilting his head to the left.

"That's a big ball of twine," Lilo said.

"Biggest ball of twine Stitch has ever seen," Stitch agreed, tilting his head to the right as he continued to stare.

"Is only ball of twine you have ever seen," Jumba said, scratching his head. "What even is twine? What is point of having big ball of it? And what is point of us making specific trip just to look at it?"

"The point is to spend time together," Lilo

replied. "It's spring break, and Nani thought we should get out of the house and have some fun!"

"And she put *me* in charge!" Pleakley said, leaping out of the RV. "I rented this recreational vehicle so we could go on an amazing field trip around Hawai'i! Plus, it'll be a great bonding experience."

"Do you really think so?" Lilo asked.

Pleakley leaned down and whispered in Lilo's ear. "No idea. All I know is your sister said that life's a little weird right now, and if I knew what was good for me, I'd take care of you while she was at work."

He wasn't kidding. It had been only a few months

since Lilo Pelekai and her big sister, Nani, had met Stitch, aka Experiment 626. Created by the alien scientist Dr. Jumba Jookiba, Experiment 626 was designed to be bulletproof, fireproof, and capable of processing information faster than a supercomputer. He could see in the dark and move objects three thousand times his own size, and his only instinct was—and we quote Jumba on this—to destroy everything he touched.

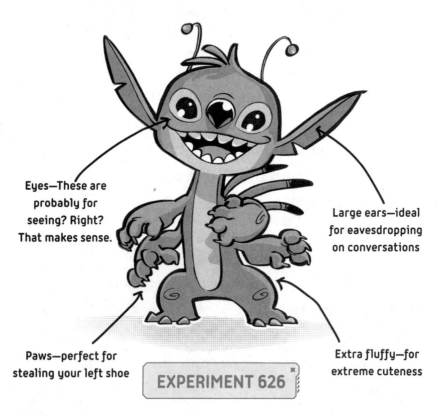

Eyes—These are probably for seeing? Right? That makes sense.

Large ears—ideal for eavesdropping on conversations

Paws—perfect for stealing your left shoe

EXPERIMENT 626

Extra fluffy—for extreme cuteness

"I think it's a *lot* weird," Lilo said, smiling at Pleakley. "And I like it."

"Same," Stitch said as he looked at the ground around the RV and saw a large frog staring up at him.

"Just think how different things would be if I hadn't adopted you from the animal shelter," Lilo said. "I never would have met real live aliens from outer space!"

Jumba turned his head and looked at Lilo. "I think what you're trying to say is 'Thank you, Jumba, for creating Experiment 626 in first place and for getting arrested by Galactic Federation, which in turn caused Experiment 626 to escape to Earth and disguise self as dog."

Stitch remembered perfectly the moment when they had adopted him. Lilo had not had any clue about Stitch's alien heritage. At first she'd just thought that he was a badly behaved pooch. That made him a great match for Lilo, because sometimes, as Stitch soon discovered, she was a badly behaved little girl. But somehow, the two seemed to bring out the best in each other.

"A really *weird* dog," Pleakley said as Lilo walked over to Jumba and gave him a big hug. The hulking alien scientist raised a single eyebrow, and to Jumba's great surprise, he hugged her back.

"Thanks, Jumba," Lilo said. "And don't worry. I forgive you for trying to capture Stitch, too."

Jumba looked slightly uncomfortable. "It was just job," he said with a sheepish shrug. "Nothing personal."

"He's right," Pleakley chimed in. "If we had not been under direct orders from the Grand Councilwoman of the Galactic Federation to subdue Stitch and bring him back into custody, we wouldn't even be here!" The one-eyed alien was the Federation's so-called Earth expert. He had accompanied Jumba to Earth in pursuit of Experiment 626. After numerous human disguises and several failed attempts to catch Stitch, Jumba and Pleakley were relieved of their duty and replaced by Captain Gantu, a hulking, no-nonsense alien with a very bad attitude. He looked something like this:

Captain Gantu

You've probably figured out by now that Captain Gantu failed, too. Otherwise you wouldn't be reading this book. It turned out that Stitch wasn't so bad after all, so the Grand Councilwoman allowed him to stay on Earth with Lilo and her sister.

Also, the Grand Councilwoman didn't want Jumba and Pleakley back anytime soon, so they ended up living on Earth, too.

Speaking of whom, both Jumba and Pleakley now found themselves standing on opposite sides of the Biggest Ball of Twine on Kauai, with Stitch positioned in the middle. Jumba tugged at the collar of his Hawaiian shirt while Pleakley primped his wig with a flourish. Since their arrival on Earth, Pleakley had taken to wearing what he believed to be stylish dresses, and an even more stylish wig. They were his Earth disguise, and he blended in perfectly.*

"A little to the left!" Lilo said, holding her camera.

"If I move any more left, I'm going to fall off ledge," Jumba said.

He was right, because for whatever reason, the Biggest Ball of Twine sat right next to the edge of a very steep cliff.

"Here, switch places," Jumba said as he picked up Pleakley, moving him closer to peril.

"Watch the dress!" Pleakley exclaimed. "It wrinkles easily!"

Stitch watched the bickering, doing his best to stay still. He was determined to make this field trip go perfectly. While Stitch had settled into his life on Earth after finding his 'ohana, or family, with Lilo, Nani, Jumba, and Pleakley, he still hadn't *quite* managed to control his destructive tendencies.

Every time he tried to help, he seemed to lose focus. It wasn't his fault that making a minor explosion in the kitchen was more entertaining

* He did NOT blend in perfectly.

than waiting for dinner to cook, or that it was fun to use his teeth to pull out the garden weeds (and flowers, and trees, and basically anything around him), or that Nani didn't appreciate his using her freshly laundered T-shirts to create a zip line through the house, or that . . .

Well, you get the idea.

"I wish I could get the ball of twine at a better angle," Lilo said, squinting at the giant display. "Oh, well. Say cheese!" She was just about to snap the photo when Stitch had an idea for how to help Lilo get the picture she wanted.

He picked up the Biggest Ball of Twine and lifted it over his head with a "Ta-da!"

Except Stitch underestimated his own strength, and when he grabbed the Biggest Ball of Twine, it flew out of his hands.

Before his friends could be bowled over, Stitch ran and shoved everyone out of the way. Then he jumped up and scampered over the rolling ball, leaping off just as it went over the cliff's edge.

"That was close!" Pleakley said as his wig flipped around. "How do I look?"

"What were you thinking, Stitch?" Lilo pointed a finger accusingly at the alien.

Stitch looked down at the ground. He couldn't bring himself to meet Lilo's eyes. All he'd wanted was to help Lilo and do something nice for her. But he'd ended up destroying the picture. Just like he *always* destroyed things.

As Stitch struggled to think of something to say, a high-pitched ringing sound came from Pleakley's purse.

Reaching into the bag, Pleakley retrieved what looked like a small compact mirror. It was, in fact, a galactic communicator. He kept it with him at all times so he could call his mom. Pleakley opened it, and his jaw nearly hit the ground.

"Grand Councilwoman!" Pleakley gasped.

"Agent Pleakley, I am contacting *you* because Experiment 626 does not *have* a galactic communicator," the Grand Councilwoman said in a no-nonsense voice. Her stern face stared at Pleakley from the communicator's screen.

"She means you, Stitch," Lilo said.

Stitch brightened a little, his curiosity overshadowing his guilt, and bounded over to Pleakley's side.

"Stitch here!" he said. Then, without warning, a glimmering beam of light pierced through the clouds, striking them all.

CHAPTER 2

CONFIDENTIAL

THE GDA

CONFIDENTIAL

"TWINE!" Pleakley shouted before realizing where they were.

The light from the beam had dazzled Stitch for a moment. As his vision slowly adjusted to normal, he saw they were no longer in Hawai'i. Instead, they were inside a sleek metal room, dotted on either side with circular portholes. Through them, he could see outer space. And standing at the end of the room, with hands folded together, was the—

"Grand Councilwoman!" Lilo exclaimed. "Is everything okay, ma'am?"

"Oh," the Grand Councilwoman said with surprise in her voice. She had only ever briefly interacted with Lilo, after going to Earth to retrieve Experiment 626 before deciding to let him stay with the Pelekai family. "So polite. Yes, well. I'm sorry about using the IMDARB* without warning. You're probably wondering why I had your molecules disassembled, sent halfway across the galaxy, and then reassembled here aboard my ship."

"I am slightly curious," Jumba replied.

"You must understand that what I'm about to tell you is of the utmost secrecy. Tell no one, trust no one," the Grand Councilwoman continued. "The Federation has discovered something disturbing on your planet. We have reason to believe that a problem of extraterrestrial origin has taken root on Earth."

"What is problem?" Stitch asked.

"We're . . . not sure," the Grand Councilwoman

* Inter-Molecular Disassembly And Reassembly Beam

replied. "But we think it might involve a renegade species of creatures known as . . . Snailiens."

"*Snailiens?*" Pleakley shouted from behind Stitch. "Not Snailiens!"

"What's a Snailien?" Lilo asked.

"I don't know! Probably something not great!" Pleakley answered.

"The Snailiens hail from the planet Gastropodia," the Grand Councilwoman said. "We know little about them. The federation assigned the Galactic Detective Agency to investigate."

"Detective agency?" asked Stitch.

The Grand Councilwoman nodded. "The Galactic Detective Agency, or the GDA, as we call ourselves, is a group of operatives assigned to investigate mysteries around the galaxy. We sent one of our best agents to look into the situation on Earth, but we lost contact with him earlier today."

The Grand Councilwoman swiped her hand over a small control panel, and a hologram appeared before them, forming a figure Stitch recognized instantly.

"Cobra Bubbles!" Lilo gasped.

Cobra Bubbles had been the social worker assigned to look out for Lilo before she met Stitch. He had helped convince the Grand Councilwoman to allow Stitch to stay on Earth and had checked in on the family periodically ever since.

"Yes," the Grand Councilwoman confirmed. "Agent Bubbles has been working for the GDA for some time. In his last communication from France, he said that he had suspicions that the Snailiens were working on a most sinister plot, but he required more evidence before he could make his move."

"Evidence?" Stitch said.

"Yes, evidence," the Grand Councilwoman replied. "We cannot act without evidence. The facts. Proof of wrongdoing. The GDA requires this. And with Agent Bubbles missing in Paris, the Federation and the GDA need someone to investigate the Snailien situation. And I need someone who I can trust. Someone smart. Someone who cannot be easily destroyed. And also, someone who is already on Earth, because we cannot afford to send any of our top operatives. Stitch, you are that someone."

"Wow!" Lilo said, patting Stitch on the back. "Does this mean you're going to be a detective?"

"Yes, if Stitch agrees, he will become an official operative of the GDA," the Grand Councilwoman said. She turned to Stitch. "What do you say? Will you help us?"

Stitch's eyes widened. He had seen TV shows with detectives during his time on Earth. They were all so smart, so heroic. This was his chance to show everyone that he was more than just a little engine of destruction. He could do this. He could be a detective!

He nodded. "Stitch accepts."

The Grand Councilwoman smiled and clapped her hands together. "Excellent," she said. "From this moment on, he will be known as *Agent 626*. I will send you off with the file on the Snailiens and with the exact coordinates of Agent Bubbles's last known location. You are to proceed at once. Find Agent Bubbles, uncover the Snailiens' plans, and put a stop to them."

"What about us?" Lilo asked. "Can we go, too?"

The Grand Councilwoman took a moment to

think and then slowly nodded. "Lilo, I know how resourceful you are and how clever you can be." She looked back at Stitch. "Agent 626, Lilo will be your assistant."

Stitch smiled and nodded in approval.

"What about me?" Pleakley protested. "I want to be a detective, too!"

"You're our Earth expert, Mr. Pleakley, so you should be familiar with this phrase: Don't push it."

The Grand Councilwoman moved toward Stitch. "As an official agent of the GDA, you'll want to familiarize yourself with this." She handed him a belt with a sleek silver case attached.

Stitch looked at the belt and scratched his head. He wondered for a moment if it was food, but then he remembered that, unfortunately, not *everything* was food.

"What is it?" Lilo asked.

"This is your Detective Tool Belt. It's the latest in mystery-solving gear," the Grand Councilwoman said. "Inside, you'll find all manner of devices that should prove useful on this assignment."

Stitch looked at the tiny silver case attached to

the belt. Roughly the size of one of Stitch's paws, it hardly seemed big enough to hold anything a detective might need.

As if in answer to his befuddlement, the Grand Councilwoman said, "It's a remarkable feat of engineering. The case is much larger than it appears on the outside. Go on, reach inside and see for yourself."

Stitch shrugged and lifted the top of the case, which opened with a click of the clasp. He stuck his paw inside and pulled out what looked like a magnifying glass and a high-tech camera. Both of the items were much bigger than the tool belt compartment. He set the objects to the side, reached inside the case again, and pulled out a cage big enough to hold someone twice his size! Then he stuck his paw inside one last time and came out with an even larger butterfly net with a silver handle.

"That's neat!" Lilo said.

Stitch nodded in agreement, though he wondered why he'd need a butterfly net. But then he thought about it for a second and imagined this:

"Do we all get one?" Jumba asked.

The Grand Councilwoman shook her head. "I'm afraid not. It's for GDA agents only. Mad scientists need not apply."

"I am not mad," Jumba grumbled. "Overly enthusiastic, perhaps."

Stitch snickered and wrapped the Detective Tool Belt around his waist. It fit perfectly. He put the magnifying glass, the camera, the butterfly net, and the cage back inside and closed the lid.

"Use that wisely. Though the case on your tool belt is rather large on the inside, it can't hold everything, so you will need to be careful. You don't want to run out of space at the most crucial point of your mission," the Grand Councilwoman said sagely.

"And next . . ." The Grand Councilwoman leaned forward and carefully handed something else to Stitch. It was the shape and size of a business card and glowed a light blue. Stitch stared at it, inspecting the object at every angle. But no matter how hard he looked, he could not figure out what it was or what it could possibly be used for.

"This is your Galactic Detective Agency badge It has all of your credentials. It will identify you as an official agent of the GDA and serve as a useful resource for you while you are on the case. Now, if you press it like so . . ."

She tapped the badge in the middle. Suddenly, there was a faint beeping sound, and a light blue hologram of a book appeared right above it. Here, you can see it for yourself:

"It allows you to look at the *GDA Official Handbook*. I suggest you study it. It also contains the case file for this mission and a guide to Earth that may serve to be useful during your investigation. Keep it with you at all times," the Grand Councilwoman said. She tapped the badge once more, the image of the book vanishing, and handed the glowing badge to Stitch.

"We wish you all success, Agent 626. Good luck," the Grand Councilwoman said. And with that, she activated the IMDARB.

FILE XG-331DNM: SNAILIENS

SPECIES: Snailien (Snailius gastropodus)

HOME PLANET: Gastropodia

KNOWN CRIMINALS: Zoolox

ABILITIES: Produces dangerous substance known as "Snail Slime." Can use handlike appendages at the ends of their antennae to hurl slime at enemies. Able to stick to almost any surface. Nearly indestructible. Has the ability to eat copious amounts of pancakes.

WEAKNESSES: Subjects appear vulnerable to a mixture of sucrose and dihydrogen monoxide combined with 5,5–dimethyl–2,4–dioxo–1,3–oxazolidine–3–carboxamide that is heated to a temperature of 115°C, beaten into a foam, and pressed into a pellet–like form. (It is believed the people of E–arth refer to these as "marshmallows.")

THREAT LEVEL

| 0 | 10 | 20 | 30 | 40 | 50 | 60 | 70 | 80 | 90 | 100 |

CHAPTER 3

A peculiar thing about the IMDARB—not only can it disassemble, transport, and reassemble atoms across a galaxy, but it can also transport those atoms through time.

What does that mean, exactly? Simply that when Lilo, Stitch, Jumba, and Pleakley arrived back on Earth, it was like no time had passed at all. Stitch looked around, scratched his head, and saw the RV.

"Well, Agent 626? What's our first move?" Lilo asked.

Stitch looked at his assistant. "Find Cobra Bubbles!"

"Great idea," Lilo said. "But didn't the Grand Councilwoman say that he was last seen in Paris? How are we going to get there?"

Stitch thought about this for a moment, which looked a lot like this:

As Stitch continued to think, Jumba tapped Lilo on her shoulder.

"What's wrong with him?" Jumba said. "Is he okay?"

"Stitch? Oh, he's fine," Lilo replied. "He's just thinking about how we're going to get to Paris."

"Paris?" Pleakley said, as if realizing for the first time what was going on. "We can't actually go to Paris! Your sister entrusted *me* with your safety! I took a sacred oath!"

Stitch looked at Pleakley and raised an eyebrow as if to say, *Really?*

"Okay, maybe not the sacred oath part, but I promised!"

"But what about the mission?" Lilo protested.

"Yes, what about mission?" Jumba chimed in. "Is very important."

"Absolutely not, no way!" Pleakley said. "It's too dangerous for Lilo and, by extension, me!"

"But we have to go!" cried Lilo.

The three of them continued to argue. They were too busy fighting to notice that Stitch had scampered away to the RV.

A few moments later, Stitch let out a loud cough. "Ahem!"

Everyone stopped yelling and turned to see that Stitch had transformed to show all four arms and his back antenna. He pressed a bright red button on the side of the RV, and THIS is what happened:

"What—what was that?" Pleakley asked in disbelief.

"Stitch may have just modified the RV so it can fly," Lilo said.

"Not 'may have,'" Jumba said. "Did. Completely did."

"It's a rental!" Pleakley screamed. "You have to return it in the same condition! This. Is. Not. The. Same. Condition!"

"Stitch can put it back the way it was after Paris," Jumba replied. "See? All details covered. Now, onward to Paris!"

Pleakley looked like he was in a daze. Stitch walked up to his friend and took him by the hand. Then he led him toward the RV.

"Is all okay," Stitch said. "Agent 626 make sure nothing happen to Lilo."

"And what about me?" Pleakley said.

Stitch stared at Pleakley, then shrugged. "Sure, you too," he said.

Pleakley wasn't reassured.

A part of Stitch wondered if Pleakley was right—if the mission was too dangerous for Lilo. But then he remembered that at this very moment, Cobra Bubbles was in trouble. Cobra had been instrumental in stopping Captain Gantu from taking Stitch as a prisoner. He really cared about Lilo, too. At the very least, Stitch owed Cobra. Even more, as an official agent of the GDA, Stitch had a duty to help.

"Woo-hoo!" Lilo shouted. "Next stop, Paris!"

The group piled into the RV, and Stitch jumped behind the controls of the converted vehicle. A moment later, they blasted off into the sky.

CHAPTER 4

CONFIDENTIAL

PARIS

CONFIDENTIAL

"Why are there no peanuts on this flight?" Jumba asked, shifting in his seat.

"Allergies," Lilo said. "You never know who has them. Better safe than sorry."

"Say, I can see everything from up here!" Pleakley said, sticking his head up into the observation bubble. "Clouds! More clouds! Clouds that look like . . ."

"Clouds?" Jumba asked.

"I was going to say mosquitoes," Pleakley replied.

"Everything looks like mosquitoes to you," Jumba sighed.

"Well, I *am* widely regarded as the number one mosquito expert in the Galactic Federation," Pleakley bragged.

Stitch looked out the window and saw the ocean below. The minute he boarded the RV, he had plugged the coordinates provided to them by the Grand Councilwoman into the vehicle's onboard navigation system and engaged the autopilot so he could review the case file the Grand Councilwoman had given him. This was his big chance to prove that he was more than just a destructive creature, and yet he didn't know the first thing about detective work.

"Are you okay?" Lilo asked, tapping her friend on the shoulder.

Stitch looked away from his reading and saw Lilo staring at him with concerned eyes. "Stitch fine," he lied.

"Well," Lilo said, "you know, maybe now would be a good time to look at the handbook the Grand Councilwoman gave you."

Stitch brightened. That was an excellent idea! He swiped the hologram of the case file, and it was replaced with an image of the *GDA Official Handbook*. He flicked the cover with his claw, and the pages turned.

"Look," Stitch said. "Detective rules!"

Sure enough, Stitch had opened to a page outlining all the rules for being a detective. Here, take a look!

RULE #1
Wherever you go, look for clues.

RULE #2
Collect evidence, but don't touch it
or you'll spoil it.

RULE #3
A good detective knows when to
detect—and when to run.

RULE #4
Be patient! Don't rush into a situation.

RULE #5
When in doubt, spit it out.

RULE #6
Just because something appears
obvious, that doesn't mean it isn't
true.

RULE #7
Be resourceful. Use what you have
around you to your advantage.

RULE #8
Always take a closer look: you may
notice something new.

RULE #9
Have a plan! (Even if it's not a great
plan, it's still better than no plan.)

Stitch stared at the rules, scratching his head. They made sense for the most part, he thought. Maybe. Sort of. He gave them another look, then dug into the Detective Tool Belt. After rummaging around, he pulled out a pair of binoculars.

"I think I understand most of these," Lilo said. "I'm not sure about rule number five, though. Why would you be putting stuff in your mouth?"

Lilo turned to look at Stitch as he shoved the binoculars into his mouth.

Lilo just stared at him.

"Stitch sorry," the alien replied, swallowing. "Hungry."

"New rule: no eating anything from the Detective Tool Belt," Lilo said.

Stitch nodded. It sounded like a good rule to him. Then he dug around the silver case some more and pulled out a circular device that resembled a compass.

"What's that?" Lilo asked.

Stitch wasn't sure. He held the device in the palm of his hand, and suddenly, a holographic map appeared above it.

"Hey, that's a map showing where we are!" Lilo exclaimed. "According to this, we just flew over Florida, and we're heading over the Atlantic Ocean now."

"Surprising how fast these new recreational vehicles are," Jumba observed.

It was only an hour or so later when the RV arrived at its destination. The vehicle circled over Paris for a few minutes as Stitch looked for the best place to land.

Suddenly, there was a loud beeping sound. It was coming from inside the Detective Tool Belt around Stitch's waist! He reached inside and pulled out the compass-like device. Stitch touched the surface, and a map of Paris appeared—with several green lights flashing in different locations. Above each green light were the words *Snailien sighting*. But the brightest light was glowing at the Louvre, a world-famous art museum.

"We're close," Stitch said.

"Better set the RV down," Lilo advised.

"Roger!" Stitch said as he maneuvered the vehicle toward the Jardin du Palais-Royal. It was a large lush green park right in the middle of the city, just north of the Seine River. Because it was still so early in the morning, there didn't seem to be anyone around yet. This was a good thing, considering a flying RV was about to burst out from the clouds and land right in the middle of the park.

"Paris at last!" Jumba shouted, taking a deep breath of air as he lumbered down the stairs, with Stitch following close behind.

"Aloha!" Stitch yelled, all four arms outstretched. Agent 626 failed to notice that he had jumped right in front of a rather elegantly dressed businessman walking with a cane. The businessman's eyes widened at the sight of the blue alien. He let out an ear-piercing shriek and ran off.

"You can't do that, Stitch!" Lilo said, hurrying to him. "Not with four arms! You'll frighten everyone! As long as there are people around, we need you to pretend to be a dog. Can you do that?"

Stitch tilted his head to one side, then nodded. He grunted and groaned as he willed the extra arms to retract inside his body.

Then he hopped down on all fours and looked at Lilo. "Bow," he said. "Wow."

"Is hard to believe anyone could mistake him for dog," Jumba said.

Just then, an older woman wearing a pair of big cat-eye glasses walked by and exclaimed, *"Oh mon dieu! Quel chien mignon!"*

Since you may not speak French, we'll translate for you. She said, "Oh my goodness! What a cute dog!" (And because you may not speak French, any other French you see in the rest of this book will be translated into English. Don't worry: we won't charge you any money for this service.)

The woman ran over to Stitch and started to pet him. She gave him a large smile, revealing rows of perfectly white teeth behind her glossy red lips. But there was something about the woman that Stitch didn't like. He couldn't put a paw on it. There was just something . . . strange. He growled at her, teeth bared.

"What a little fighter he must be!" the woman said, still petting Stitch. "So full of life!"

Before Stitch could do anything else, Lilo put herself between him and the fancy French woman. She offered her a polite smile. "His name is Stitch. He would really like to see some art. Do you happen to know the quickest way to the Louvre museum?" she asked.

"Why, you're practically on top of it!" the woman said with a broad grin, her white teeth glinting in the sunlight. "It's just a few blocks that way, on Rue de Rivoli!"

In case you didn't know, *rue* in French means "street."

"Thanks, ma'am. That's very helpful. Have a nice day!" Lilo said, waving as she walked off in the direction of the museum, with Stitch, Jumba, and Pleakley following close behind.

"Goodbye!" the woman said, waving her gloved hand in the air.

"Bye," Stitch replied.

"Such a well-mannered little dog," the woman observed.

CHAPTER 5

"Since when does Stitch love art?" Pleakley asked as they walked down the city street toward the Louvre museum.

"Since Stitch detect Snailiens," Stitch said. He held up the compass-like device for the group to see. "With this."

He handed the compass to Pleakley. The hologram map appeared. The green dot on the Louvre was even brighter than before.

Stitch stopped walking and sniffed. Then he sniffed again. His supersensitive nose had caught an odd scent. Stitch was reminded of one of the detective rules:

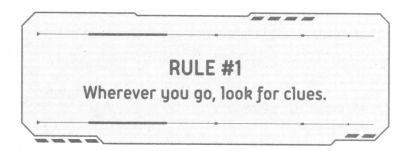

RULE #1
Wherever you go, look for clues.

A moment later, Stitch pressed his nose to the ground, sniffing like a bloodhound as he crawled ahead on all fours.

"I take back what I said before about dog disguise," Jumba said. "Experiment 626 is doing best dog impression I've ever seen."

Lilo ran ahead of Jumba and Pleakley, catching up to Stitch. "What do you smell?" she asked.

Stitch sniffed once more, then looked at Lilo. "Smell like popcorn," he said. He looked around. There was no popcorn to be seen. But as his attention turned toward the ground, he spotted something else: a faint trail of something green.

He crawled over to it and gave it a big whiff. It

was definitely the source of the strong popcorn smell!

Stitch reached into the silver case and pulled out the magnifying glass. He looked at the green ooze through the lens, and this is what he saw:

Stitch couldn't believe it! He had found a real clue! He moved forward, following the trail of green Snail Slime. Lilo stayed right on his heels as they weaved through a passing crowd.

"Lilo, wait! Don't go ahead without us!" Pleakley called out from behind them. He and Jumba tried to catch up, but it was too late. Stitch and Lilo were on the move!

Stitch sharply turned the corner and continued to follow the trail until he came across a big puddle of bright green goo in the middle of a dark alley. The smell of fresh, buttery popcorn was over-powering.

"Snail Slime!" Stitch exclaimed, pointing at the gross, icky stuff.

Stitch was about to reach out and feel the slime when Lilo cried, "No! You can't touch that, Stitch. It's evidence!"

At Lilo's words, Stitch recoiled. He opened his tool belt, pulled out his badge, and clicked it to bring up the *GDA Official Handbook*. With a swipe over the holograph, he opened the book right to the rules page.

RULE #2
Collect evidence,
but don't touch it or you'll spoil it.

Stitch wanted to follow all the GDA rules. He needed to prove to everyone on this mission that he had what it took to be an amazing detective. So Stitch rummaged through the silver case for a moment, then pulled out a plastic vial with a stopper on top.

"Great thinking, Stitch," Lilo said, beaming at him. "You can use that to scoop up some of the Snail Slime. But you have to be gentle, or you'll break it."

Stitch held the vial in his right paw. He was used to breaking things, because breaking things was easy for him. But holding something and not breaking it? *That* was hard. Still, he did his best, and with extra care and caution, he scooped up a bunch of the glowing green Snail Slime in the plastic vial.

But before Stitch could place the evidence safely into his silver case, a strange sound came from behind a garbage dumpster.

SCHLORRRRRRP · · ·

CHAPTER 6

CONFIDENTIAL

SNAILIEN SIGHTING

CONFIDENTIAL

As Stitch whipped around toward the source of the sound, a big glob of green goo sailed past his head and splatted against a brick wall behind him. And then he saw it: a creature, easily twice his size, with two bright yellow eyes, glaring at him from the entrance to the alleyway. Two antennae sat atop its head, and the thing's entire body glowed, shrouding the dark space with a sickly green light.

Suddenly, the creature's antenna extended, gripped a nearby trash can, and hurled it at Stitch.

"Snailien!" Stitch shouted as he moved out of the

way of the trash can. He grabbed Lilo and held her over his head, jumping on top of a dumpster.

"That thing's pretty gross!" Lilo said, and she wasn't wrong.

SNAILIEN *

Stitch and Lilo slid off the top of the dumpster just as the Snailien unleashed another barrage of green slime.

"Give . . . me . . . that . . . vial!" the Snailien snarled, indicating the silver case on Stitch's belt. "We cannot allow you to take any evidence of our presence on this planet!" One of his antennae lashed out, snaking behind the dumpster, trying to snatch the case from Stitch.

It was then that Stitch remembered another detective rule:

RULE #3
**A good detective knows
when to detect—and when to run.**

"Time to go!" Stitch shouted, and the pair darted from behind the dumpster and around the Snailien.

"You can't get away from me!" the Snailien said. To Lilo and Stitch's surprise, the Snailien sprouted three legs beneath his slimy body and came at them even faster!

At the end of the alley was a chain-link fence. Stitch knew he could climb it in no time flat, but Lilo? Not so much. Then he remembered what had happened back at the Biggest Ball of Twine.

"Lilo!" Stitch said as the Snailien approached. "You trust Stitch?"

"Always!" she said.

"Hold on!" Stitch said. He picked up Lilo and threw her over the fence. She sailed right over. Then Stitch squeezed his arms through the open spaces between the metal chain links and caught Lilo before she hit the ground.

The Snailien was almost upon him as Stitch started to climb. But he noticed something on the ground next to him: a pair of dark sunglasses. He grabbed them and shoved them into his tool belt, then climbed over the fence, escaping the Snailien.

Or so Stitch thought.

The Snailien ran into the chain-link fence. But instead of being stopped by it, the Snailien simply oozed right through it!

"What is going on here?" Pleakley screamed. He and Jumba had run around the other side of the alley and joined up with Lilo and Stitch. "This looks like something that's going to get me in trouble with your sister!"

"It's Snailien!" Stitch said as he pulled Pleakley out of the way of the creature's antenna. The end of the antenna smashed against the sidewalk where Pleakley had been standing, sending pieces of concrete everywhere.

Stitch urged the group forward as the Snailien continued to pursue them. He knew they needed to get away from the creature, and they also needed to go to the Louvre. As they raced down the sidewalk toward the museum, they ran past a fruit cart.

Thinking fast, Stitch broke away from the group, darting over to the cart. The vendor looked at Stitch and smiled. Then Stitch said, "One banana, please." (He remembered to say *please*, because manners, even during a Snailien chase, are very important.)

The vendor handed a banana to Stitch, who reached inside the silver case and pulled out a coin with the Grand Councilwoman's face on it. "Here you go," Stitch said. "Space money!"

"Merci," the vendor said.

Stitch ran back to the group as the Snailien

came even closer. He peeled the banana before
throwing the mushy inside at the Snailien.

SPLAT!

It hit the creature right between the eyes. The surprised Snailien stopped and let out a high-pitched scream.

"Argh!" the creature roared, recoiling from the attack. "I am hit by some kind of devastating Earth weapon!"

With the Snailien distracted, Stitch, Lilo, Jumba, and Pleakley hurried away and entered the Louvre museum.

Inside the museum, the gang hurried through the entryway. They were forced to separate as a gaggle of visiting elementary school students heading in the direction of the gift shop scurried between them. Stitch ran as fast as his paws would take him, with Lilo following close behind. They were racing past all kinds of fancy art displays. Stitch thought it would have been nice to actually stop and look at the art if he'd had some time. As it was, there was one painting in particular that caught his eye:

At least, that's how Stitch remembered it looking.

Anyway, no matter where they ran, the Snailien followed on his three gross, slimy legs.

"Give me back the sssslime!" the creature wailed as museum guests casually walked out of his way. No one seemed to care about the sudden appearance of this monstrous, snail-like creature. Nor did they seem to notice that a blue "dog" was running around on its hind legs at an impressive speed.

"Performance art," one guest sniffed.

"Been there, done that," said another.

As the Snailien chased Stitch and Lilo through the museum halls, he left a thick trail of slimy green goo.

"Gross!" Stitch said. He ducked around a corner, pulling Lilo with him. They could see the Snailien's back as the creature looked around to try to find them.

"You said it, Stitch," Lilo agreed. "It's totally gross! But how are we going to get away from that thing and get our slime sample to the Grand Councilwoman?"

Stitch thought for a moment, and then suddenly he had an

IDEA!

"Snailien wants slime sample," Stitch said. "Give slime sample to Snailien!"

"What? Give it to him?" Lilo exclaimed. "Stitch, we can't just give it to the Snailien! If we do, then we can't analyze it! It's the only clue we have to find Cobra Bubbles and discover what the Snailiens are doing here."

But Stitch didn't listen to her. Instead, he ran right toward the Snailien! With a jump, he grabbed a nearby painting and used it to surf the long trail of slime.

He reached down to the floor and scooped up a big handful of gooey green Snail Slime. Hearing Stitch's approach, the creature snarled and turned to face him. That was when Stitch hurled the slime right in the Snailien's face!

WHHH AAAAAA MMMMM!

"Gah!" the Snailien shouted as the slime hit his eyes, temporarily blinding him. "First, that horrible, devastating Earth weapon! And now, thwarted by my own precious slime! How embarrassing!"

"Time to go!" Stitch shouted, and he and Lilo took off.

Less than a minute later, they had found their way back to the bustling museum entrance and through the front doors . . . as a pair of hands reached out to grab Lilo!

CHAPTER 7

CONFIDENTIAL

AGENT TROUBLE

CONFIDENTIAL

"Pleakley!" Lilo shouted as the one-eyed alien held on to her shoulders.

"Lilo! Thank goodness you're okay," Pleakley said, his wig askew on his head. "If Nani finds out what happened, no place on Earth will be safe for me!"

"Hurry! Snailien coming," Stitch said, looking behind him. The Snailien was trying to make its way to the museum entrance but was blocked by a passing tour group.

"Get in there," Pleakley said, pointing at a taxicab waiting for them on the nearby street.

Lilo, Pleakley, and Stitch packed themselves into the back seat of the taxi. The vehicle was already driving away as Stitch closed the door behind him.

"What were you thinking?" Pleakley screamed.

"First you say, 'Hey, let's go to Paris!' and then, what do you know, you converted the RV into a flying monstrosity! And then we arrive in Paris, where you run off, and suddenly, there's a green, gooey . . . thing chasing after us!"

"Is not 'thing,'" Jumba corrected him. "Is Snailien. 'Thing' is something else entirely."

Snailien ≠ Thing

"Whatever! The point is I was right! This is waaaaaay too dangerous for Lilo," Pleakley said. He turned his attention to Stitch. "You guys just ran off without any warning! Do you know what could have happened to you back there with that Snailien? And if something happened to you, what could happen to me? I'm the babysitter! No one ever thinks about what could happen to the babysitter! A Snailien is nothing compared to an angry Nani!"

At first Stitch didn't say anything. He looked at Lilo and then out the window. Here he was, trying to show everyone that he was Agent 626, detective, and he had put his best friend in danger. *That* was something Experiment 626 would have done, not a professional detective. Finally, he said, "Stitch agree."

"Wait, you do?" Pleakley said, surprised.

"Yes," Stitch said. "Is all Stitch's fault."

"Not all," Lilo protested. "I went along with it. So if you're going to punish Stitch, you have to punish me, too."

"*Punish* you?" Pleakley said, flustered. "I can't punish you! If I punish you, your sister's going to say, 'Why did you punish Lilo?' Then I'm going to have to tell her *why* I punished you, and if I do *that*, she's going to punish *me*!"

Stitch looked at Pleakley, not knowing what to say. He knew the mission was dangerous, but the Grand Councilwoman wouldn't have transported them across the galaxy and back and enlisted their help to solve the mystery of Cobra Bubbles's disappearance and discover what the Snailiens were planning if it weren't important.

He was just about to say something when Pleakley waved his hand. "That's it," Pleakley said. "Trip is over! We are done. Back to Hawai'i, everybody!"

"But we can't—" Lilo interjected.

"Oh, we *can*," Pleakley said. "And we will. Right, Jumba?"

"Hmmm?" Jumba said, distracted. "Sorry, was not paying attention."

The taxicab pulled up to the curb outside Jardin du Palais-Royal, and the driver turned around, holding out her hand.

It was clear that she was waiting for her fare,

but Jumba said, "Is nice hand." Then he got out of the car.

Everyone piled out after Jumba and followed him back to the RV—the RV that had a parking ticket on the window.

"Great," Pleakley said, tearing the ticket from the windshield. He waved it frantically in Lilo's face. "Now, on top of everything else, we got a ticket! We're criminals in France! How will I be able to live with myself knowing that I am a wanted alien?"

"Is not so bad. I'm criminal practically everywhere in galaxy, and look at me," Jumba said, puffing up with pride.

Pleakley groaned. "That's it. Everyone into the RV," he said, pointing to the door. "The sooner we leave this cursed city, the sooner we can all go back to our normal lives. This detective business has been nothing but trouble."

With that, he trotted up the RV steps, followed by Lilo and Jumba.

And Stitch?

Stitch slogged in behind them, barely lifting his feet or his head as he thought over Pleakley's words. He wondered if Pleakley was right—if he really was nothing but trouble. He had been trying so hard to be a good GDA agent, but it seemed that he had already failed. The scene in the alley, the museum . . . all of it was just a big mess.

Stitch slid into the driver's seat. His nose twitched, and for a moment, he thought he could smell popcorn. Then he put the key in the ignition and turned it. Instead of the familiar sound of the engine starting, there came a loud, familiar

CHAPTER 8

CONFIDENTIAL

AMBUSH

CONFIDENTIAL

"What was *that*?" Pleakley screamed, leaping out of his seat.

Slowly, a green slime oozed out of the ignition. A second later, the key shot out like a cannonball, hitting Pleakley right in the eye.

"Ow!" Pleakley cried.

The green slime dripped onto the RV floor. As the pile grew, it became thicker and grosser, until standing right in front of Lilo was a horrifying Snailien, even bigger than the one that had been chasing them at the Louvre!

"Give us our slime!" the Snailien said.

"Get out of our RV!" Lilo countered.

"Is technically not 'our' RV," Jumba corrected her. "Is rental."

Stitch turned to look at the RV door and saw another gooey green Snailien pressed up against the window outside, blocking the only exit. The alien was making some kind of goofy face at him, which Stitch didn't appreciate. So he made a goofy face right back.

When the Snailien backed off, Stitch rubbed his chin thoughtfully. What would a detective do in this situation? Then he remembered another rule:

RULE #4
Be patient! Don't rush into a situation.

Stitch realized that either he could try to fight his way out—like the old 626—or he could wait, observe the scene, and follow through, like Agent 626, the new Galactic Detective Agent he wanted to prove to everyone he could be.

"What do we do?" Pleakley said. "Panic? Is panicking an option?"

"Panicking is *always* option," Jumba said calmly, rolling his eyes at the other alien. "And you are *very* good at it."

"Guys! Focus!" Lilo said. She picked up a tennis racket and waved it threateningly at the Snailien. "Stay back! I'm warning you. I know how to use this thing!"

"Your Earth weapon is indeed fierce and mighty!" the Snailien said, advancing on Lilo. "But what we lack in weapons we make up for in numbers!"

"In numbers?" Lilo said, and as she turned her head around, she saw green goo pouring in through the seals around the windows until four Snailiens were inside the RV!

"RV is surprisingly roomy," Jumba observed.

"Brothers and sisters, attack!" the Snailien commanded, and the aliens began to close in.

"Where's Stitch?" Lilo said, waving the tennis racket at a Snailien. "I don't see him anywhere!"

Unfortunately for Pleakley, in the second he took looking for Stitch, the Snailien—SCHLORP!— sucked his head right into its mouth.

"Hey!" Pleakley shouted in a muffled voice. "I'm using that!"

Lilo smacked the Snailien in the stomach with her tennis racket. The Snailien coughed and spat Pleakley right out.

"My hair!" Pleakley cried, touching his head. His wig was covered in green Snail Slime.

"You know who we are," the Snailien continued. "You know *what* we are. And if you take that slime to the Galactic Detective Agency, they will analyze it. In time, they might discover our mission. And that we cannot allow. The Plan must succeed."

"Plan?" Lilo said. "What plan?"

"Do not speak of The Plan, Doobor!" a Snailien standing next to Jumba shouted. "You've said too much!"

"Zoolox warned us—no first names, Gooblo!" Doobor ordered. Immediately, he covered his mouth with his antenna. "Gasp! I've broken Zoolox's rule!"

"Did he just say 'gasp'?" Jumba asked. "Why not just gasp? Is better to do than to say."

"You understand nothing, Jumba Jookiba!" Gooblo said.

"How—how did you know his name?" Lilo asked.

"We know who you are," Doobor sneered. "We know that you have been sent by the Grand Councilwoman! We know many things."

"For example, we know that something has happened to Meebort!" Gooblo said, pointing at the RV door.

"Again with the first names thing?" Doobor said. Suddenly, he realized what Gooblo was saying. Looking outside, he said, "Why has Meebort left her post?"

With a gross SCHLORP, Doobor oozed to the windshield and looked outside. But when he got there, all he could see was:

CHAPTER 9

"Get! That! Thing!" Doobor commanded as the other Snailiens scrambled for the windshield.

"How'd he get out there?" Pleakley squeaked.

"Always the surprises from 626," Jumba said, genuinely impressed.

From outside the RV, Stitch looked at the Snailiens as they crowded in around the driver's seat. Then he stuck out his tongue and went,

"THBBBBBBBBBBBBBBBBBB."

Very disrespectful. Also, funny.

A second later, Stitch was gone. He scrambled along the top of the RV, then down to the bottom.

The RV had a large luggage compartment set into the back that connected to the inside of the vehicle. Stitch popped it open with his claws and dove in. With incredible speed, he scampered around the suitcases and bags. He paused for a moment by the inside hatch, reaching into the case on his tool belt. Stitch remembered something from the file the Grand Councilwoman had shared with them. Something about a weakness . . . He pulled out a stapler, which he decided was useful but not really appropriate to his situation. He tossed it back in and next pulled out a penguin.

Stitch patted it on the head gently and set it back inside the case. At last, he came up with exactly what he was looking for.

A moment later, the door to the luggage compartment on the inside of the RV burst open and Stitch jumped out. And he was ready for battle!

"Stitch!" Lilo shouted in surprise.

"My tie!" Jumba shrieked.

"Eat marshmallow!" Stitch said, squeezing the triggers on his blasters.

Marshmallows flew through the RV, hitting Gooblo.

"Oh, no!" he wailed. "Snailiens are powerless to resist marshmallows! They are so delicious, and our bodies cannot help absorbing them! And once we do, we fall asleep, adrift in sugary dreams of delicious white fluff, and are unable to eat any more of our source of nutrients—pancakes!"

"Gooblo!" Doobor said, staring at the Snailien. "Do not continue to further explain our weakness!"

"My bad," Gooblo replied.

Stitch tossed one of the blasters to Lilo, who caught it and started firing at Doobor.

"Get them out of the RV!" Lilo shouted. She shot marshmallows at the Snailiens, forcing them toward the vehicle's exit.

Soon Lilo and Stitch were side by side, firing their marshmallow blasters at the gooey intruders until all the Snailiens were backed against the door.

"You think you have us beat," Doobor snarled. "But your marshmallows won't last forever! And when you run out, that's when we'll attack! And then, when we are victorious, we will eat your marshmallows! What do you think about that? Huh?"

"I think you haven't been paying attention," Lilo said.

"Huh?" Doobor replied as Stitch jumped right at him, holding the bag of marshmallows.

"Quick, brothers and sisters!" Doobor said, his eyelids drooping. "We must leave this place before I fall into the slumber of marshmallow dreaminess!"

The other Snailiens scrambled to Doobor's side and picked him up before fleeing out the RV door.

"This isn't over," Doobor said as he let out a big yawn. "This . . . isn't . . . overzzzzzzzzzzzzzzzzzzz. . . ."

"We did it!" Lilo whooped, and turned around to high-five Stitch.

"Where did you get those marshmallow blasters?" Pleakley asked.

Stitch smiled at Pleakley and patted the silver case on his belt. Then he put the marshmallow blaster back inside—but not before firing a few dozen marshmallows into his mouth.

"So are we going to stop the Snailiens or what?" Lilo asked.

"Oh, you *bet* we're going to stop them. They got slime in my wig!" Pleakley said. "You know, that was really something back there. You might be the best detective I've ever met."

Stitch grinned.

"Is only detective you ever met," Jumba said grumpily. "Also, I'd like my tie back."

CHAPTER 10

CONFIDENTIAL

THE TRAIL

CONFIDENTIAL

Stitch thought briefly about eating Jumba's tie, not so much because it looked delicious to him (it did) but because he just wanted to see what Jumba would do. But that was very much an Experiment 626 thing, and he was trying hard to be a good GDA operative.

Speaking of which, at that particular moment, the Grand Councilwoman appeared on the RV's windshield, like a head-up display. "Agent 626!" she said urgently. "Do you have any information about the Snailiens?"

"Yes," Stitch said. "Stitch have information. And Snail Slime!"

He retrieved the glowing vial of evidence from the Detective Tool Belt and held it up for the Grand Councilwoman to see. Her eyes lit up.

"We have never been able to procure a sample of Snail Slime! Not even Captain Gantu could obtain any. And yet here you've done it," the Grand Councilwoman said, grinning. "You are full of surprises, Agent 626." Stitch beamed. There was nothing he liked more than outdoing Gantu.

Stitch: 1
Gantu: 0

"Now, if you set the vial of Snail Slime down, I will send an IMDARB beam to retrieve it. The scientists at the GDA will analyze the sample. Perhaps it holds a clue as to the whereabouts of Agent Bubbles," the Grand Councilwoman said.

Stitch put the vial on the floor of the RV and then backed away. A moment later, there was a flash of light, and the vial was gone!

"One more thing . . ." Stitch said.

"That's right," Lilo said, jumping in. "The Snailiens mentioned something about 'The Plan.'"

"The Plan?" the Grand Councilwoman replied. "What plan?"

"They didn't say," Lilo added. "Doobor's exact words were 'The Plan must succeed.'"

"This is indeed disturbing news," the Grand Councilwoman said. "We will get back to you as soon as we have information about Agent Bubbles. In the meantime, Agent 626, I need you to find out more about this 'Plan' before the Snailiens can cause any more harm."

"Stitch on the case!" the alien said proudly, and then he started to gag.

"Are you all right?" the Grand Councilwoman asked.

A moment later, Stitch coughed up the binoculars.

"Gross," Lilo said.

"We are in agreement," the Grand Councilwoman said, nodding at Lilo. "Now go, and report back!"

The view screen dimmed as Stitch looked at his friends through the binoculars.

"I guess that's the fifth rule of being a detective," Lilo said.

"Stitch! Can I borrow your binoculars?" Lilo asked, and Stitch was polite enough to wipe his drool off before handing them to her. If Stitch knew anything, manners were important. This is how he imagined he looked when he was on his best manners:

"Am I the only who thinks that's disgusting?" Pleakley asked.

Before anyone could answer, Stitch jumped as if he'd suddenly remembered something. He headed to the door of the RV.

"What's wrong, Stitch?" Pleakley asked.

"Nothing's wrong," Stitch said as he scampered out the door and pointed at the grass. "Snailien trail!"

Sure enough, there was a very faint path of glowing green slime!

Lilo moved up behind him and held the binoculars to her face as she looked in the direction of the trail.

"It looks like it continues that way," she said, gesturing forward.

Stitch put a paw on his chin thoughtfully as he leaned over to examine the slime. "Hmmmmm," he said. Then he put his chin in his other paw and said, "Hmmmmm," again. Something just didn't seem right to him, but he couldn't quite put a claw on it.

"What? What is it?" Jumba asked.

Stitch shook his head. "Slime goes that way," he said, pointing, as he continued to think about the scene before them.

"Yes? So?" Jumba replied.

"But Snailiens go *this* way," Stitch said, pointing in the opposite direction.

"How do you know?" Lilo asked.

Stitch sniffed, and his nose twitched as he inhaled the familiar scent. "Popcorn," he said. "Snailien smell."

"So the slime trail is just a decoy?" Lilo asked.

Stitch nodded. A second later, his nose was smooshed against the ground, sniffing, as he walked quickly in dog mode, chasing the Snailiens' scent.

"All right, people," Lilo said. "Everyone follow Stitch! He'll lead us right to the Snailiens!"

With Stitch in the lead, Lilo, Jumba, and Pleakley followed, tracking the Snailiens through the streets of Paris. In case you were wondering, it looked something like this:

START

Many cats, pigeons, and mosquitoes later, the intrepid group found themselves standing in front of the Palais Garnier, a historic opera house. Stitch scratched his head.

"Are you sure your nose is right?" Lilo asked, squinting up at the old building.

Stitch looked at Lilo and snorted. "Stitch nose *always* right."

"But why would Snailiens be hiding in opera house?" Jumba argued. "Does file say anything about them enjoying dramatic compositions in which all dialogue is sung to instrumental accompaniment?"

"Maybe they're music lovers!" Pleakley suggested, scratching at his mosquito bites.

"Or maybe they chose this hiding spot so they could scare people away!" Lilo said.

"What does little girl mean?" Jumba said.

Stitch looked at Lilo and nodded, reaching inside the Detective Tool Belt. He retrieved his badge and pressed it. A second later, the *Galactic Federation Guide to Earth* appeared above, and Lilo flipped through the pages until she found what she was looking for.

"See? It says here in the section on Paris that the Palais Garnier was the setting for Gaston Leroux's famous 1910 novel, *The Phantom of the Opera*! Maybe the Snailiens are haunting the opera just like the Phantom did in the book!" Lilo exclaimed.

"I don't know, Lilo," Pleakley said with a doubtful look. "That seems kind of . . . obvious."

"Just because something's obvious doesn't mean it isn't true," Stitch declared.

RULE #6
Just because something appears obvious, that doesn't mean it isn't *true*.

"Perhaps little girl and 626 are right," Jumba said. "I say this because they might be right, and also, puddle of green slime by front door."

CHAPTER 11

CONFIDENTIAL

THE OPERA

CONFIDENTIAL

Stitch, Lilo, Jumba, and Pleakley hurried inside the Palais Garnier, along with a group of well-dressed opera fans decked out in tuxedos and fancy dresses. To say that our friends stood out like a sore thumb wouldn't begin to describe it. Here, see for yourself!

They made their way through the crowd, and as Lilo's eyes darted left and right, she realized that she had lost sight of Stitch.

That is, until she heard a woman exclaim in a loud voice, "My goodness, it's that unusual yet cute dog from this morning!"

Running among the crowd of people, Lilo found Stitch near the doors that led to the theater itself. He sniffed the ground next to the woman from the park, who was still wearing the big cat-eye glasses.

"Why, hello!" the woman said upon seeing Lilo. "I didn't know that dogs were allowed in the opera. But it makes sense, considering how delightful your little friend is."

Stitch sniffed the woman's leg and then let out a growl.

"Thanks, ma'am," Lilo said, scooping Stitch up in her arms. "I hope you enjoy the opera."

"I'm sure I will," the woman said. "I hope you and your exceedingly strange dog do, too!"

Stitch narrowed his eyes at the woman as Lilo hurried back to the group.

"Hey! You can't just run off like that!" Pleakley whispered.

"What's wrong with you, Stitch?" Lilo asked.

"Why were you growling at that nice lady?"

"Stitch smell something," he said. "Popcorn!"

Jumba pointed to a nearby concession stand.

"There is your popcorn smell," he said.

"They sell popcorn at the opera?" Pleakley said, delighted. "Let's get some!"

Stitch frowned. He had been sure he had smelled a Snailien! He would need to be more careful.

Lilo pointed to the theater entrance. "I bet the Snailiens are in there," she said, heading toward the open doors.

An usher with slicked-back hair and a raised eyebrow blocked Lilo's path. "Tickets, please," she said.

Jumba looked at the usher, then turned to face Lilo. "What is ticket? I am scientist. Is that not worth price of admission alone?"

They moved to the side as the usher continued to take guests' tickets. Stitch looked around and saw another usher open a nearby supply closet. Stitch remembered detective rule #7:

RULE #7
Be resourceful. Use what you have
around you to your advantage.

Then he smiled and said, "Be right back!"

"Stitch, wait!" Lilo said, but it was too late. Stitch bounded off, scampering right behind the usher, who was fumbling inside the closet, looking for a mop and a bucket.

"Hi," Stitch said with a little wave of his hand.

"Follow, please!" Stitch said as he walked right past Lilo, Jumba, and Pleakley and to a door leading to the main floor of the opera.

"No one's going to believe he's an usher," Pleakley said, shaking his head.

"Do not underestimate 626," Jumba said. "He can be very persuasive."

The usher standing by the door took one look at Stitch and raised her eyebrow. "And just where do you think you're going?" she asked.

Pleakley gulped, sure that they had been caught.

"Look at you!" the usher continued. "Your uniform is far too large. You are a disgrace to the profession."

Stitch nodded, and Pleakley looked like he might pass out.

"Seat your guests, then fix your appearance," the usher said as she walked away from the door.

Jumba turned to Pleakley and smiled from eye to eye.

Stitch raced down the aisle, sniffing the floor, with Lilo, Jumba, and Pleakley close behind. The operagoers who had already been seated stared at the little usher as he took the group all the way to the front of the theater.

"Well?" Jumba asked.

Stitch sniffed the air, trying to distinguish the smell of Snailien slime from the popcorn guests were eating. Finally, he pointed to the stage. "Trail go back there."

"Behind the stage?" Lilo said. "Of course! According to Leroux's book, there are tunnels beneath the opera house. *Secret* tunnels! And a big lake! I bet *that's* where the Snailiens are hiding!"

"There's a lake?" Pleakley asked. "Beneath the opera house? This planet is full of wonders!"

"And right now, I'm wondering how we can get back there," Lilo said.

But Agent 626 was already on the case. He walked right up to the stage manager standing next to a door that led backstage.

"Excuse me. This area is off-limits," the manager said, frowning at Stitch over his square glasses.

"Tourists," Stitch said. Then he jerked a thumb

behind him, toward Lilo and the group. "They want to see backstage."

"There are no tours before the show," the stage manager said. He waved Stitch away. "Now go make yourself useful."

Stitch looked up at the stage manager, who was now actively ignoring him. Then he jumped on him, holding on to his coat, and smiled right in the stage manager's face. Just like this:

"Tour," Stitch repeated.

"Oh!" the stage manager said, his demeanor changing. "By all means. I'm sorry to keep you waiting."

He stepped aside as Stitch let go and landed on the floor. The alien led everyone through the door.

"E-enjoy your t-tour!" the stage manager called after them.

CHAPTER 12

The trail led them to an unmanned door below the theater. As soon as the group walked through it, Pleakley gasped. "There really is a lake!"

"Sure there is!" Stitch said. He touched the detective badge, and the *Galactic Federation Guide to Earth* appeared once more.

"It says here that the builders of the opera house discovered that the Seine River flowed underneath the location," Lilo said. "No matter how hard they tried, they couldn't pump the water out. So the architect Charles Garnier came up with the idea of controlling the water by making this big lake!"

"Why not just create huge monster capable of drinking all water until problem goes away?" Jumba asked.

Stitch imagined that monster would look something like this:

"Boy, creating monsters is your solution to everything, isn't it?" Pleakley said. Then he looked at Stitch and made an *oops* face. "No offense, Stitch."

Stitch frowned. He knew that Pleakley didn't really mean anything by what he'd said, but it hurt that anyone still thought of him as a monster. Maybe after they finished their mission, they would see him as a super-helpful, smart, resourceful detective.

"Maybe because the people who built the opera house didn't have access to stuff that could create a big lake-gulping monster?" Lilo suggested.

"Is good point," Jumba said, nodding.

While the others debated whether a monster would have solved Charles Garnier's problem, Stitch had moved on and was already solving another problem—namely, how to explore the lake and the tunnels beyond.

Stitch spotted two flat boats docked at the water's edge. He ran right over and hopped in.

"Hey, boats!" Lilo said. "Good idea, Stitch. Now we can investigate the tunnels and find the Snailiens."

Jumba and Pleakley walked over and stood behind Lilo.

"Too many for one boat," Stitch said. "So split up."

Lilo nodded. "I'll go with Stitch!"

"Why do I have to go with Pleakley?" Jumba asked.

"Yeah, why do *I* have to go with *him*?" Pleakley repeated. "Besides, I'm supposed to make sure nothing happens to Lilo!"

"But I'll have Stitch to protect me. Besides, you two *always* go together," Lilo said. "It would be bad luck to break you up."

"I'll accept that," Jumba said. He maneuvered into the boat. The craft wobbled as he got in, and it seemed for a moment that the boat might tip over. But it settled down as Jumba sat. Pleakley followed. Stitch threw off his usher suit, got into the other boat, and sat beside Lilo.

Now that the two boats were adrift on the underground lake, Stitch took out a paddle. He saw Pleakley do the same.

"Where to, Stitch?" Lilo asked.

Stitch sniffed and caught the scent of popcorn. He said, "That way."

As the two boats paddled down the lake, Lilo could have sworn she heard the wind blowing.

Except it wasn't the wind.

Careful ears would have heard an eerie

SCHLORRRRRP · · ·

"It's cold down here," Pleakley said, shivering.

"Then paddle faster," Jumba suggested. "Will warm your body."

"Why don't *you* paddle for a while?"

"Because I am thinking," Jumba replied.

"About what?" Pleakley asked.

"About not paddling."

The gang had been searching by boat for some time and had at last come upon two tunnels.

"Which one leads to the Snailiens?" Pleakley asked.

Stitch sniffed the air and then scratched his head.

"What's wrong, Stitch?" Lilo asked.

"Snailien scent getting strong," Stitch said. "Smell popcorn in both tunnels. But no Snailiens around."

Pleakley shivered. "I'm glad about that," he said.

"If there were Snailiens around, I'd be too cold to do anything about it. And that wind! Can you hear it?"

Lilo paid close attention to the sound that had been echoing through the cavern for a while.

"Um, Pleakley?" Lilo's voice was tentative. "I don't think that's the wind."

Just then, the water began to bubble around them, and the boats rocked back and forth. The lake became more turbulent, and then . . .

Something hit the bottom of their boats!

"Is probably too late to go back, yes?" Jumba asked as he snatched the paddle from Pleakley. He started to row in the direction of the dock, but the water was now so rough it was impossible for the scientist to turn the boat around.

Then the water settled down, growing still once more.

"Well," Pleakley said, looking relieved. "I'm glad that's ov—"

Suddenly, the water exploded around them!

"Snailien!" Pleakley shouted, waving his hands in the air wildly. "Snailien!"

"Tunnel!" Stitch instructed. He used his free hand to point ahead.

The group started paddling furiously as the water roiled around them. With a SCHLORP the Snailien dove beneath the surface, the top of its antenna just peeking out above the water like a shark fin as it swam toward the boats at an alarming speed.

"Row faster! Row faster!" Pleakley said frantically, gesturing at Jumba. "It's gaining on us!"

Next to them, Lilo and Stitch paddled as quickly as they could. Then the Snailien reared up and bit off the end of Stitch's paddle.

Unable to steer, Stitch and Lilo drifted through the tunnel on the right. The Snailien tried to follow, but the opening was too small for its huge, bulbous body. The creature slammed against the entrance as bricks crumbled, dropping into the water below.

Unable to reach Stitch and Lilo, the beast turned around, eye narrowing at the remaining aliens. Jumba hurriedly switched directions and paddled rapidly toward the other tunnel.

"What are you doing?" Pleakley exclaimed. "We have to follow Stitch!"

"We can't go that way!" Jumba said. "Unless you want to get eaten!"

"I don't want to get eaten!" Pleakley said.

"Then we go left tunnel!" Jumba insisted.

With a splash, the Snailien followed Jumba and Pleakley toward the tunnel on the left. With every passing second, the creature was getting closer . . . closer.

"Hurry!" Pleakley said. He dipped his hands in the water and paddled. "Here, I'll help!"

But then . . .

"That's enough helping!" Pleakley said, placing his hands back inside the safety of the boat.

The Snailien ducked beneath the surface again, and the water calmed down. Jumba kept on rowing, his eyes focused on the tunnel ahead.

"Almost there," Jumba said. "Almost th—"

But just as the boat was about to sail through the tunnel, the Snailien burst from the water. The creature's fearsome mouth opened wide, and the Snailien swallowed the boat whole—along with Jumba and Pleakley.

CHAPTER 13

CONFIDENTIAL

THE BEAST'S BELLY

CONFIDENTIAL

You're probably saying to yourself, "Wow, Jumba and Pleakley got into some serious trouble. But what are Lilo and Stitch up to if not getting swallowed by a giant Snailien? And can I have a snack?"

Well, it's okay with us if you have a snack, but you should probably ask an adult or something. Also, take it from Stitch: binoculars are NOT a snack.

As for Stitch and Lilo, they had been rowing along the lake and through the tunnel for nearly a half hour already, with no end in sight.

"I hope Jumba and Pleakley are okay," Lilo said, taking the flashlight from her backpack. She turned it on, shining the light down the tunnel. "At least that big Snailien isn't following us. Where do you think this goes?"

Ahead of them, the tunnel curved to the right. Stitch sniffed, and his ears perked up. "Turn off light!" he said, and Lilo immediately shut off the flashlight.

"What is it?" Lilo whispered. "What do you hear?"

SCHLORRRRRRP · · ·

"It was that, wasn't it?" Lilo said.

Stitch nodded.

The boat drifted silently along, carried by the current, until it emerged from the tunnel inside an enormous cavern.

"Look!" Stitch whispered, pointing ahead.

There, on the shore, was a hulking structure that looked like the wreck of a spaceship. Around the wreckage were a group of Snailiens, all of whom appeared to be working on it.

"Aha!" Stitch said. "Snailien ship! But how it get here?"

"Maybe they crashed their ship on Earth and brought it here so they could repair it," Lilo said. "Y'know, so nobody would see them."

"Fix so they can go home?" Stitch wondered aloud.

"Maybe that's The Plan," Lilo added.

But something told Stitch that wasn't The Plan. Why would the Snailiens go to all the trouble of bringing their ship to this cavern to repair it?

They'd have to blast their way out, and they'd possibly wreck their ship again in the process. If they were really rebuilding the ship, it would be smarter to do it somewhere outside.

Stitch was trying very hard to be a good detective, but a part of him just wanted to go all, you know . . .

But he realized that was something Experiment 626 would have done. As Agent 626, Stitch couldn't just be destructive. Instead, he decided to follow detective rule #8.

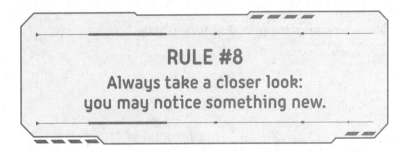

RULE #8
Always take a closer look: you may notice something new.

The boat drifted along until it hit the shore on the opposite side of the cavern, far enough away from the crashed spaceship that the Snailiens wouldn't see them. Once on shore, Stitch and Lilo crouched behind a rock and peered over it at the aliens. Now that they were closer, Stitch could get a better look at what they were doing. That was when he realized . . .

"Not fixing ship," Stitch said. "They are building something."

As Stitch and Lilo continued their investigation, and presumably as you ate a snack of some kind, Jumba and Pleakley had spent about forty-five minutes inside the stomach of a strange aquatic creature.

"You know, I expected that it would be darker in the belly of this enormous Snailien, but it's surprisingly bright!" Pleakley said.

"Glad to see you found silver lining," Jumba said sarcastically.

"I hope you're very uncomfortable," came a loud, booming voice.

"Who's that?" Pleakley asked.

"Who do you think it is?" the voice said. "It is I, Flootbar the Invincible!"

Jumba rested his chin on his hand as he dipped his other hand in the shallow water surrounding the boat. Or maybe it was stomach acid and gross stuff. Either way, he didn't seem to mind.

"Sorry, I don't know of any 'Flootbar the Invincible,'" Jumba said, sounding bored.

"Flootbar! The Invincible!" the voice repeated. "I'm feared throughout all the known galaxies! I'm big! I swim! I swallowed you whole! Including your boat!" Jumba and Pleakley couldn't see Flootbar from inside his stomach, but if they could he would look like this:

FLOOTBAR! THE INVINCIBLE!

"Oh!" Pleakley said, catching on. "You're the voice of the big Snailien that ate us!"

"Now you're getting it!" Flootbar said. "Anyway, I ate you, you're inside me, and you'll soon be digested along with everything else I swallowed today."

Pleakley turned his head and saw this:

"Is that . . . Are you . . . ?" Jumba started.

"It is, and I am," Cobra Bubbles answered, without a trace of humor.

"Aha! We did it! We found Agent Bubbles," cried Pleakley. "That will show the Grand Councilwoman! See? Stitch isn't the only one suited to being a great detective."

"Yes, yes, you can tell her after monster digests us," Jumba said dryly before turning his attention to Cobra. "What are you doing inside of Snailien?"

Cobra sighed. "Been down here for a while now, floating around inside this thing."

"Hey!" Flootbar interrupted. "Not a *thing*! I'm Flootbar! Most glorious, destructive being in the known galaxies! Look, you all might as well just settle in and get used to the idea that you're my prisoners for all eternity or until I digest you, whichever comes first."

"This day is not going as planned," Cobra said with a heavy sigh.

"Oh, they never do," Flootbar agreed.

"Don't get too close!" Lilo warned.

Slowly, Lilo and Stitch crept along the shore, hiding behind the concrete pillars that supported the roof of the gigantic cavern. They were getting close enough to the Snailiens' wrecked spaceship to get a better look at what the creatures were building.

"Any idea what that could be?" Lilo whispered, facing Stitch.

Stitch shook his head. It looked kind of familiar, whatever it was, but he couldn't quite put his claw on it.

"Maybe they're building an engine," Lilo said. "Or something they could use to power their big spaceship."

Stitch thought for a moment and shook his head again. "Is not for ship," he said. "Look. Snailien destroy ship. Use parts to build new thing."

"But if the Snailiens aren't making something for their ship, what are they doing?" Lilo asked.

Stitch wondered the same thing. Before Lilo could stop him, he scampered off, heading right for the wrecked spaceship.

CHAPTER 14

"See? I knew we could have all fit in one boat!" Pleakley said as he gestured at Cobra Bubbles, who had joined them in their ship. They were completely packed in, with their shoulders touching, barely able to move.

"I don't know if I'd call this fitting," Cobra said with a sigh.

"Excuse me, what happened to your sunglasses?" Jumba asked, pointing at Cobra's face. "Looked good on you."

"I dropped 'em right before I was captured by the Snailiens," Cobra said. "They were chasing me down an alleyway. Just gobbled me right up in one gulp, and next thing I knew, I woke up inside ol' Flootbar. And I've been stuck listening to his stories ever since."

"Ha! That's a thing that sure did happen!" Flootbar interjected. "Say, did I ever tell you about the time I ate Qwarloon the Magnificent's space pod?"

Jumba rolled his eyes. "Doubtful, as we only just met you," he said.

"Oh, I've heard this one twice already," Cobra said with a groan.

"I for one would *love* to hear about the time you ate Qwarloon the Magnificent's space pod," Pleakley said enthusiastically.

Jumba leaned over and punched him in the arm.

"Ow!" Pleakley said with a wince. "What was that for?"

"Because now, thanks to you, it's story time," Jumba said.

"Great story, right?" Flootbar said.

"Oh, great story," Cobra said. "Even better than the story you told about the time you had a really great nap."

"But I haven't told you a story about the time I had a really great nap," Flootbar replied. "I guess you must have heard about it, though, huh? It's a good one, so I'll tell it again!"

"Why are you making him tell another story?" Pleakley whispered to Cobra, adjusting the wig on his head.

"Because it keeps him busy," Cobra said. "Gives me time to think. To plan."

"Say, plans are great!" Flootbar said. "Sorry, didn't mean to eavesdrop. But wait till you find out about *our* plan. The Plan, we call it. Boy, you're gonna love it. It's an eyeful!"

Stitch crouched behind a concrete pillar and rifled through the Detective Tool Belt until he pulled out the camera. He pointed it at the device the Snailiens were constructing and pressed the button.

CLICK!

A moment later, a photo slid out from the bottom. Lilo had caught up to him, and she took the picture and waved it in the air while it developed.

"Evidence," Stitch said, pointing at the photo.

"It's great that you're collecting evidence, Stitch," Lilo whispered. "But you can't just take off like that without telling me the plan."

Stitch frowned.

"But I am proud of you," Lilo said. "When you ran ahead, I thought you were going to attack the Snailiens. You've really learned a lot about being a detective! It's like you're a whole new Stitch."

Stitch smiled at the mention of a "new Stitch." He really liked the sound of that!

"Now we go," Stitch said. "Find others and show evidence to Grand Councilwoman."

"... and that's the story of the greatest nap in the history of the known galaxies," Flootbar said. "Say, aren't you guys digested yet?"

"I wish," Jumba replied. He looked at Pleakley, who was primping his wig, and suddenly had an idea.

What, 626 is only one allowed to have idea?

"Pleakley," Jumba whispered. "Give me wig."

"What?" Pleakley said, clamping his hands down around the wig on his head. "No! It's mine! It wouldn't match your complexion anyway!"

"I don't want to *wear* wig," Jumba said, still whispering. "I need it for escape!"

"Wait, what?" Pleakley asked.

"I can't believe I'm gonna say this," Cobra whispered. "But I think I know where he's going with this."

"You do?" Pleakley replied. "Because I don't. I'm clueless!"

In the background they could hear Flootbar starting to tell another long story, which may or may not have been about the time he became the most famous staring contest champion of all the known galaxies.

"See two holes up there?" Jumba said, pointing at the top of Flootbar's stomach. "I believe those are nose holes. Like blowhole on whale. Use wig to tickle nose holes."

"Then Flootbar sneezes us out," Cobra said, nodding.

"Whoa, whoa, whoa!" Pleakley said. "You *believe* those are nose holes? What if they aren't? What if they're something worse? And what about my wig?"

"You'll get precious wig back, promise," Jumba said. "Now, are you going to give it to me to save us or what?"

Pleakley was torn. On one hand, he loved that wig more than anything on Earth. Don't believe us? Here, take a look.

On the *other* hand, he did not want to be digested inside the belly of some big gooey, evil alien snail. He slowly and gently removed the wig from his head.

"See you soon, Lucille," Pleakley whispered as he passed it to Jumba.

"Lucille?" Jumba asked.

"It's a family name," Pleakley explained.

Shrugging, Jumba took the wig and hurled it at Flootbar's nose holes.

". . . and that's the story of how I ate the best molten weernax cake—along with the bakery that made it—in the known galaxies," Flootbar said. "And now . . . wait. What's . . . what's going ah . . . ahhhh . . . AHHHHHHH . . ."

It was working! The hairs from Pleakley's wig were irritating Flootbar's nose holes. Any second now, the enormous creature was going to

"We're free!" Jumba shouted.

"Hey!" Flootbar hollered. "Come back here!"

"Lucille!" Pleakley screamed as he managed to snatch the wig in midair.

They landed in the water with a loud splash.

"What do we do now?" Pleakley asked as he put the wig back on his head.

"Swim," Cobra said. "And hope we don't have to listen to any more stories."

CHAPTER 15

EVIDENCE

"Jumba! Pleakley!" Lilo hollered, waving her arms. "Over here!"

Lilo and Stitch were waiting outside the Palais Garnier. Stitch was chowing down on a hot dog, making loud yummy sounds.

MMM

MMMMM

"How can you eat at a time like this?" Lilo asked.

"Stitch hungry," the alien said.

Jumba and Pleakley walked toward the pair, still covered in green goo. It dripped off them, and they left a slimy trail all the way from the opera entrance to the street.

"What happened to you?" Lilo asked. "Are you okay?"

"We were eaten by that giant Snailien!" Pleakley exclaimed. "And then we were trapped in its huge stomach! In retrospect, it's completely fascinating."

"Yes, but at time, was the worst," Jumba said, jumping in. "Snailien talked. So much talk. Too much talk. Long, boring stories. Was like listening to Pleakley."

"Hey!" Pleakley said.

"And look who we found!" Jumba said, stepping aside to reveal Cobra Bubbles standing behind him.

"Agent Bubbles!" Stitch cried.

Lilo jumped up and hugged him immediately. "You're okay!"

"Well, I'm not covered in snail snot," Cobra replied, and smiled ever so slightly at Lilo.

"What happened while you were captured?" Lilo asked. "Did the Snailien say anything important?"

"Well, he told us about the one time he ate Qwarloon the Magnificent's space pod, the time he had the greatest nap in the history of the known galaxies, and the time he ate the best molten weernax cake in the known galaxies, along with the bakery that made it," Cobra said without taking a breath.

"But were there any clues?" Lilo pressed him.

"Flootbar did say one thing that was peculiar," Cobra said, rubbing his chin. "He said, 'Wait till you find out about The Plan. You're gonna love it. It's an eyeful!'"

"He said that?" Lilo asked.

"Or words to that effect, yes."

Suddenly, Stitch's eyes brightened and he tossed aside the hot dog, which hit Pleakley right in the face.

"What is it, Stitch?" Lilo asked.

"Is clue!" Stitch said. "Plan is *eyeful*. EYEFUL. What does it mean?"

"Obviously, it means plan must be something extremely pleasing to eye," Jumba said. "Is not so hard to figure out."

But Stitch wasn't convinced. For one thing, it seemed too easy. For another, why would the Snailien bother to say that their plan would be great to look at?

"What?" Jumba asked, glaring at Stitch. "You don't believe greatest scientist in known galaxies? Oof, now I sound just like Flootbar."

"Yeah," Cobra said with a frown, cracking his knuckles. "You do."

"We need to let the Grand Councilwoman know that Agent Bubbles is safe," Lilo said.

"And tell her about new evidence," Stitch said, nodding in agreement.

Pleakley pulled out his galactic communicator, and Stitch held out his hand. "Please?" Stitch asked.

"Well, I'm not happy about the hot dog to the

face, but since you asked so nicely . . ." Pleakley replied, handing the communicator to Stitch.

The group moved to an alleyway on the side of the building, where fewer people could see them. Stitch pressed a few buttons, and a hologram of the Grand Councilwoman appeared above the device.

"Agent 626!" the Grand Councilwoman said. "We have information for you."

"Stitch have information, too!" Stitch said, and gestured to Cobra.

"Grand Councilwoman," Cobra said.

"Agent Bubbles! I'm so pleased to see that you're alive," the Grand Councilwoman said. "We must debrief you at once!"

"There'll be time for that later," Cobra said. "I found out some information on that . . . *other thing* you had me looking into that I think you'll want to hear. But right now, Stitch needs to give you a status update."

"We found Snailiens' ship," Stitch said. "They build something."

"But we don't know what," added Lilo.

"That's a concern," said the Grand Councilwoman. And if you knew the Grand Councilwoman, then you'd know that anytime she said, "That's a concern," that meant things were really, really bad. In other words, on a scale of 1 to 10, with 1 being the best and 10 being the worst, "a concern" was about 350.

"Uh-oh," Jumba said.

"The GDA scientists have analyzed the slime

sample you sent us," the Grand Councilwoman said. "It appears that their slime contains the exact same properties as the energy that powers the Galactic Federation's IMDARB technology."

The Grand Councilwoman waved her hand, and a hologram of the IMDARB device appeared next to her.

IMDARB

"Stitch, that looks like what the Snailiens are building!" Lilo shouted. She pulled out the picture she had taken in the cavern and held it up so the

Grand Councilwoman could get a good look. Don't worry: we'll hold it up so you can see it, too.

"That is very troubling," the Grand Councilwoman said, frowning.

"Why would they need their own IMDARB?" Lilo asked.

"Whatever the reason, the Snailiens must not be allowed to finish their creation," the Grand Councilwoman said. "Agent 626, you know what must be done."

"Roger!" Stitch said, throwing the Grand Councilwoman a salute.

"The fate of the Earth and, indeed, the entire Galactic Federation, rests in your hands," she said.

As the hologram faded from sight, Jumba raised his hand.

"Just one question," Jumba said. "How is it in all of Paris, with so much food option, 626 manages to find hot dog?"

CHAPTER 16

AN EYEFUL

CONFIDENTIAL
CONFIDENTIAL

"I'm off to debrief with the Grand Councilwoman," Cobra said. He started tapping his watch, ready to activate the homing beacon there. The beacon would direct the IMDARB to his location, transporting him across the galaxy to the Grand Councilwoman's ship.

"Wait," Stitch said. He reached inside the Detective Tool Belt and handed a pair of sunglasses to Cobra.

His sunglasses.

"You dropped these," Stitch said.

"Agent 626, huh?" Cobra said with a little grin. "Keep them. If you're gonna work for the GDA, you should look like a detective."

Stitch smiled back as he put the sunglasses on.

A second later, Cobra pressed his homing beacon and vanished in a flash of IMDARB light.

"What now?" Lilo asked.

"Go back to caverns," Stitch said. "Destroy Snailien device."

"Any ideas on how to do that?" Lilo asked.

"The Destructicon 3000!" Pleakley said, barely

able to contain his excitement. "It can destroy anything!"

"Do we have a Destructicon 3000?" Lilo asked.

Pleakley was quiet. "No," he said eventually. "Not exactly."

"We are missing obvious," Jumba said. "We have Experiment 626! Is most destructive force ever created! We unleash him, he destroys Snailiens' machine."

Stitch frowned. He had been working so hard to follow all the GDA rules and to be a great detective. And being a great detective meant not just running in and smashing things; that was what the old Stitch was known for. But now Jumba wanted Stitch to do just that. After all his hard work, did they still think that was the only thing he was good at?

"What's wrong, Stitch?" Lilo asked.

"Nothing," Stitch said with a shrug, looking down at the ground. "Let's go."

"It's gone!"

Lilo stood inside the cavern underneath the Palais Garner, staring at the wrecked spaceship. But there was no sign of the Snailiens, and the IMDARB device they had constructed was nowhere to be seen.

"This is not good," Jumba said. "Well, vacation has been fun. Perhaps time to leave Earth, yes?"

"We're not going anywhere," Lilo said with grit in her voice. "We're gonna find those Snailiens and stop 'em. Right, Stitch?"

"Hmmm? Yes, stop 'em," Stitch said, distracted.

"Can you track the Snailiens? Smell where they went?" Pleakley asked.

But Stitch said nothing. Instead, he was thinking. Not about what Jumba had said before—but about something Cobra mentioned that Flootbar had said, about The Plan. About how it would be an "eyeful." Stitch was positive that it had nothing to do with an amazing sight. It had to mean something else. But what?

That was when it hit him.

Stitch pulled out his GDA badge and pressed it. The *United Galactic Federation Guide to Earth* appeared once more.

"What are you doing, Stitch?" Lilo asked.

The alien flipped through the pages on the device furiously, looking for something. At last, he came to this page:

"Aha! Not 'eyeful,'" Stitch said. "'Eiffel.' Eiffel Tower!"

"Oh, that makes more sense than other thing," Jumba said.

"That must be where the Snailiens are headed," Lilo said. "We have to get there and stop them before they can use the IMDARB for their plans."

"Perfect opportunity to harness 626's destructive properties!" Jumba said with obvious enthusiasm.

Stitch grew quiet again, his ears drooping by his face. This time, Lilo noticed. She put her arm around him.

"What's wrong, Stitch?" she asked. "Really?"

"Stitch more than just smash things," he replied sadly. "Stitch want to be great detective."

"You *are* a great detective, Stitch!" Lilo said. "Wait, is that what you think? That we just want you to break things?"

Stitch gave a sheepish nod. "It all you think Stitch good at."

"That's not true," Lilo said. "Stitch, you have been a great detective. We never would have come this far without you."

"She's right," Pleakley said.

"Grudgingly, I have to admit this also," Jumba added. "I made you to be perfect engine of destruction, 626. But you are so much more. Every day, you prove this. Truly, you are amazing detective."

"And we need you, Agent 626," Lilo said.

Stitch looked up at his friends. He didn't know what to say. This was all he wanted—to be recognized as something more than just a destructive monster. He had set out to prove that he could use his brain and be a detective. And he had done that. Now it was time to do more.

"Let's go!" he said, leading the group out of the cavern. "Time to stop Snailiens!"

CHAPTER 17

When Stitch and his friends emerged from the Palais Garnier, it was dark outside.

"What's the fastest way to the Eiffel Tower?" Lilo asked. She was already glancing at the street, looking for a taxi that could take them.

"Stitch know," the alien said, and then he took out the keys to the RV.

"Wait, does he have pockets?" Pleakley asked.

"626 is full of surprises," Jumba said.

Stitch pressed the red button on the key fob, and it made a rapid BEEP BEEP sound.

Less than thirty seconds later, a high-pitched whine could be heard overhead. Everyone turned to look as the RV swooped in and hovered above them.

"Everybody in!" Stitch said.

It took the RV less than a minute to reach the Eiffel Tower. The tower's yellow lights glowed bright against the night sky, and Stitch could see that a crowd of people was assembled on the ground below.

"Going in for a closer look," Stitch said as he guided the RV down. He expertly piloted the vehicle, getting as close as he could without hitting anything. Stitch noticed that the spectators on the ground were pointing at the tower, confusion written across their faces.

Squinting, Stitch followed their eyes to see what had caught their attention. Upon closer observation, not all the lights appeared to be their usual yellow. Some of them were a sickly green.

"Snailiens!" Stitch shouted, pointing.

Sure enough, there were Snailiens swarming around the Eiffel Tower, leaving trails of glowing green slime.

"Hang on!" Stitch said as he took the vehicle in for a landing. The RV hit the grass, and the intrepid group rapidly exited.

"What's the plan?" Lilo asked.

"We don't need plan," Jumba said flatly. "Goal is to stop Snailiens."

But Stitch remembered the last detective rule.

RULE #9
Have a plan! (Even if it's not a great plan, it's still better than no plan.)

"That is not plan," Stitch said. "That is mission. Plan is . . . Stitch know what plan is. Follow me!"

The little blue alien raced into the crowd of people that had surrounded the Eiffel Tower. They were all so busy pointing at the strange glowing green blobs that they didn't even notice Stitch or the other aliens.

"How do we get up there?" Jumba asked. "Is not like we can just take elevator."

"Why not?" Stitch asked.

"I'll tell you why not," Jumba said. "Is because . . . because . . . because it is entirely reasonable idea."

"Great, so we're agreed—elevator it is!" Lilo said as she dashed through the esplanade beneath the massive wrought iron tower. The guest elevators were set inside three of the four pillars that supported the structure. The group made their way to the east pillar, and Lilo pressed the up button.

The elevator doors opened, and the group piled inside. Lilo noticed Stitch was not among them.

"Stitch!" she shouted.

"Stitch meet you up there!" Stitch shouted from outside the elevator. "Trust me!"

"Always," Lilo said as the door between them began to close. "But where are you going?"

That's a great question! Where *is* he going, anyway? He's somewhere in this picture, but if you're really curious, we guess you could just keep reading the book, too. Right? That's always an option.

CHAPTER 18

Stitch scrambled up the wrought iron framework of the Eiffel Tower, using his alien arms to climb up the building silently and swiftly. He wanted to know exactly how many Snailiens there were, and he wanted to see where they had set up their IMDARB device. Then he would meet Lilo and the others and come up with a proper plan.

The trip up the framework wasn't easy. Stitch had to constantly twist and turn, ducking around the supports to avoid being spotted by the Snailiens.

"Our work is almost done!" said one Snailien as Stitch snuck past them. He recognized the creature as Doobor from the attack on the RV. "Soon this world will glow green with our slime!"

"Yes!" another Snailien agreed. Stitch recognized this one from the RV, too: it was Gooblo. "This tower will make the perfect antenna to broadcast our transportation beam across the known galaxies to our home planet—Gastropodia!"

Stitch's eyes widened. So *that* was what their plan was! They were going to bring more Snailiens to Earth. It would be an invasion!

Stitch took note of the two Snailiens and continued his climb up the structure. He realized that the aliens weren't just oozing around the Eiffel Tower for fun. They were dragging wires behind them and connecting them at intervals to the tower itself.

Unfortunately, while he was busy noticing that, Stitch *didn't* notice the splotch of green goo right in front of him. Not in time, anyway. He put his right hand on it and slipped!

Falling, Stitch managed to catch himself with

one of his extra arms, which he sprouted just in the nick of time.

"Snailiens," Stitch grumbled, shaking the slime off his fur. "They the worst."

The elevator doors opened on the second floor, and Lilo poked her head out, looking left and then right.

"So far, so good," Lilo whispered. "No sign of any Snailiens. The IMDARB must be on the third floor!"

"But elevator only goes to this floor," Jumba said, pointing at the controls.

"There must be another that will take us up there," Pleakley said. "Unless you want to walk up the stairs."

As the group left the elevator car, Lilo saw something move from the corner of her eye. Her gaze shifted toward the stairs as she saw a little tuft of blue fur poking up.

It was Stitch!

She was just about to call out to him when Stitch peeked his head out. He pressed a claw to

his mouth, making a
SHHHHHHH gesture.
Then he pointed up.
And that was when
Lilo saw this:

"What do we do?" Pleakley said.

"We can start by not doing anything," Jumba whispered. "Don't make a move."

Lilo turned her head and looked at Stitch. He winked at her, and then he ducked down, disappearing from view.

"Where he goes?" Jumba asked. "Now would have been good time to go all, you know, Stitch."

"Don't worry," Lilo said. "Stitch has a plan."

Jumba looked up at the Snailiens, who were so occupied with attaching the wires to the metal beams that they had yet to notice him or the others.

Then Pleakley sneezed.

ACCCHHHHOOOOO!

The loud noise drew the Snailiens' attention, and they gazed down at the hapless Pleakley, their eyes glowing with fury.

"Whoops," Pleakley said. "Sorry. Just ignore me. Nothing to see here!"

"How even can you sneeze?" Jumba bellowed. "You don't have nose!"

"Let's worry about that later," Lilo said. "We have bigger problems right now!"

The Snailiens slid down the wrought iron beams, and—SCHLLOOORP SCHLOORRRRRRP—moved closer and closer to the group.

"You don't belong here," one of the Snailiens said.

"Zoolox would be most displeased to see you," another Snailien added. "So we will make sure that he *never* sees you."

Then the Snailiens laughed, and if you've ever heard a Snailien laugh, then you'll believe me when I say that it sounds like someone slowly letting the air out of a thousand balloons: a terrible high-pitched whining sound, coming in fits and starts.

And if you've *never* heard a Snailien laugh, then you'll just have to take our word for it.

As the Snailiens closed in, Lilo, Jumba, and Pleakley formed a tight circle, their backs against each other.

"Whatever Agent 626 has planned, I hope he does it fast," Jumba said.

"Me too," Lilo said.

Well, it certainly does look like everyone's in trouble, doesn't it? I mean, not you and me; we're great. I'm talking about Lilo, Pleakley, and Jumba specifically. Y'know, if only they were friends with an incredibly smart and resourceful space detective, that might help.

Oh, hey, what do you know? They are! Well, what are you waiting for? Turn the page and find out what happens next!

CHAPTER 19

The Snailiens were almost on top of Lilo, Pleakley, and Jumba, their large round eyes narrowed. Just as they were about to close in on the group, suddenly, four wires, flung like lassos, grabbed on to them. Lilo watched in astonishment as the four Snailiens were pulled back. With a loud snap, the wires suspended them in midair, leaving the Snailiens dangling above the group like piñatas dangling from a tree.

It was Stitch!

"I am floating!" one of the Snailiens said, a twinge of panic in their voice.

"I also am floating!" another Snailien wailed.

"We are *all* floating!" cried the third. "And yet, I also have the strangest feeling that something is holding on to us!"

Slowly, almost in unison, the Snailiens rotated their heads around and saw Stitch. His feet were braced against the metal beams while he held on to the wires the Snailiens had been using to attach their IMDARB device to the Eiffel Tower.

"Well, this explains the floating feeling," a Snailien said.

"Yes, and the feeling of something holding on to us," another replied.

"Amazing work, Stitch!" Lilo said, and Stitch beamed with pride.

"It nothing," Stitch said as he tied the ends of the wires around a metal beam. Once they were secure, he leaped down and landed next to his friends. Then he looked up at the Snailiens dangling overhead.

"Okay, Snailiens," Stitch said as he got right in one of their faces. "Where IMDARB?"

"We'll never talk!" the Snailien said. "Never! Go on, do your worst. Snailiens are famous throughout the known galaxies for our ability to keep our mouths shut!"

Stitch nodded politely, then reached behind him. He casually grabbed hold of one of the nearby metal beams and tore it off. All color drained from the Snailien's face as Stitch . . . well, as he did *this:*

"Snailiens are also famous for our ability to talk when it will keep us alive!" the Snailien babbled, quickly changing their tune. "We'll tell you what you want to know. Just don't eat us!"

Stitch grinned. That was when he realized there was another detective rule:

RULE #10
Sometimes you just have to unleash your inner Stitch!

"All right, Snailien," Lilo said. "Talk!"

"The IMDARB is at the top of the tower," the Snailien said. "But you'll never reach it! The others have disabled the elevator. And the device itself is heavily guarded by our most fierce warrior! He is big! And strong! And big!"

"You said 'big' twice," Jumba pointed out.

"That's for emphasis," the Snailien continued.

"We need to find a way up there," Lilo said. "Maybe we can reason with their leader."

"Zoolox cannot be reasoned with!" one of the captured Snailiens said. "That is why they call him Zoolox the Unreasonable!"

That's me!

Zoolox the Unreasonable

"Well, we're going to try, anyway," Lilo insisted.

"But how do we get up there?" Jumba asked. "Elevator is not working."

"What about the stairs?" Pleakley asked.

Jumba turned his head to look at Pleakley. "Do I look like I want to take stairs?"

"I'm guessing . . . no?" Pleakley replied.

"No stairs," Stitch said. "Get in elevator."

"Are you sure about this, Stitch?" Lilo asked.

The group stood inside the elevator, doors closed, with Stitch on top of the car. He dug the claws on his feet into the roof of the elevator car, and then he sprouted another set of arms from his sides and grabbed the cable with all four of his paws.

"Stitch sure!" he said, and then the alien began to climb the cable, paw over paw over paw over paw.

Slowly, the elevator car moved up.

"This . . . this is safe, right?" Pleakley asked.

"Is safe as anything else we've done," Jumba noted with a shrug.

Pleakley didn't look so good.

CHAPTER 20

THE PLAN

In case you were wondering how long it takes a little blue alien to pull a full elevator car up to the top of the Eiffel Tower, it takes about ten minutes. Maybe eleven, because Stitch had to stop to scratch his nose. (In all fairness, it was really itchy.)

When the car finally came to a stop, Stitch squeezed the emergency brake tight around the cable, stuck the elevator in place, and joined his friends inside the car.

"What's the plan, Stitch?" Lilo asked.

Stitch reached into his Detective Tool Belt, produced a crumpled piece of paper, and unfolded it. Here's what he came up with:

STITCH'S PLAN

1. stitch distract shailiens!
2. Lilo reasons with ZOOLOX!
3. Jumba and Pleakley turn off IMDARB!
4. EVERYONE have SNACKs!

"Hmmm," Jumba said. "Is good plan. Especially snacks part."

"All right, then let's do this," Lilo said. "Stitch, we're counting on you."

Stitch gave a sharp nod, then wedged his paws in between the elevator doors. Effortlessly, he pried them open, and the gang exited onto the third floor.

Looking around, Stitch spotted the IMDARB device. Countless wires were plugged into it, draped all around, connecting it to the Eiffel Tower. There were four Snailiens guarding it, but curiously, there was no Snailien at the controls.

Only . . . *her*.

"Oh, I see you've finally joined us, Agent 626," the woman wearing the cat-eye glasses said. "Better late than never, I suppose."

Everyone's jaw dropped. Stitch recovered first. Suddenly, the random encounters with the woman in the park and at the opera didn't seem so random. That was when Stitch finally realized what was going on. "Hello, Zoolox," Stitch said.

"Zoolox?" asked Lilo.

"Bravo," the woman said. She pressed a button on the inside of her glove. The disguise of the fancy woman in the large glasses flickered away. In her place stood Zoolox, with his proud unibrow and sinister monocle. "I knew when Flootbar captured Agent Bubbles that the GDA would be sending more of you to interfere with our plans, so I used this hideous human disguise to watch you! I'm guessing you'd like to stop me from activating the IMDARB, thus opening the doorway between Gastropodia and this world, finally allowing us to have a proper home! Soon your Earth will be overrun with Snailiens, and *then* where will you be? Huh? Huh?"

"Still here?" Stitch replied.

"Yes, obviously, but I meant that in a broader sense!"

In that moment, Stitch decided he'd liked Zoolox better when he'd thought the Snailien was a fancy French woman. He didn't understand what Zoolox was talking about, and he didn't care. So Stitch did what any reasonable, rational being would do.

BLEAH
BLEAH
BLEAH

"That does it! Snailiens! See that our little friend doesn't interfere with our plans!" Zoolox ordered as he turned his attention back to the IMDARB.

The other Snailiens advanced on Stitch. They started to make weird throaty sounds. Then they spat green goo right at Stitch! He managed to duck out of the way as bright green blotches went SPLAT all around him. Wherever the goo struck, the metal began to melt!

"Since when can they do that?" cried Pleakley.

"Remember plan!" Stitch yelled as he dove over the side of the tower. The four Snailien guards followed, clinging to the metal beams with their slime as they slid after him.

"Right, the plan," said Lilo. She cleared her throat and walked over to Zoolox, who had gone back to the IMDARB. "Mr. Zoolox, may I speak to you for a moment?"

Zoolox turned away from his work, his unibrow furrowed. "Look, I don't have time for this. I have a planet to conquer! Yours! I just want to be really clear about that."

"There has to be some way we can work this out," Lilo said. "You don't need to conquer Earth. We could be friends, you know?"

"Hmmm . . . let me think about that," Zoolox said. "No."

Lilo asked, "Why do you even want to invade Earth?"

"Because we discovered this!" Zoolox said. He thrust a flyer in Lilo's direction.

"But why can't you just make pancakes on Gastropodia?" Lilo asked.

"Have you ever *been* to Gastropodia?" Zoolox said. When Lilo shook her head, he continued. "You're not missing anything."

While Lilo did her best to reason with Zoolox the Unreasonable, Stitch clung to the metal beams with his claws, climbing as fast as he could to keep the other Snailiens away from his friends. As he crawled, blobs of green Snail Slime hit the metal beams all around him, melting whatever they touched.

"Hey! How about you stay still so we can hit you?" one of the Snailiens said.

"Yeah! That would sure make our job easier," added another.

"No thanks," said Stitch. He wondered how long he could keep scrambling along the tower. The Snailiens were relentless and had a never-ending supply of Snail Slime. Maybe it was time for a new plan.

Right then, Stitch knew what he was going to do. He turned to face the Snailiens, his feet digging into the metal beam. Then he ran toward them as fast as his legs could take him.

"What—what is he doing?" a Snailien said.

"Fire!" another Snailien said. All four creatures made awful noises like they were about to spit, and then they unleashed a torrent of Snail Slime. Stitch ducked and dodged as best he could, but

d r l   ea   h Zoolo

le, tit   clu

eam ll a und m,

cl

"   w ab   yo

e Sn

he c   ep scr

         Sli   e. Maybe it

        d. Sl

      est he co ld.

W   bes to rea   wit Zoo x
                   ng   e metal b   ns
               as fast   ne   d to   o
               fr   e
               1
         him,

to
               ay st l s

                    e our job

               . He wonde
he   g th ower. Th
  aliens   d ha   never-end
  pply   nail Slime. M   it   ne   a new
lan.
    bt th

ue n
his leg

"   ar
   ed and

Whoa! Sorry about that. Snail Slime tends to get everywhere, you know? So let's try that again, hopefully this time without the mess.

As the Snail Slime went SPLAT all around Stitch, he managed to avoid it all. Finally, he was right in front of the four Snailiens. At first, he did nothing, just standing there as the Snailiens, antenna drooping, huffed and puffed, worn out from their attack.

Then, at last, Stitch said one word in a calm voice.

"Boo."

The Snailiens lost it. They shrieked and slid all the way down from the top of the Eiffel Tower to the esplanade below and landed with a

SPLAT!

"Stitch still got it," Stitch said, puffing up his chest in pride.

He smiled, looking over the side of the tower at the Snailiens as they ran off. Then Stitch had the feeling he was being watched. He slowly turned around.

"Hello!" came a loud, booming voice. "Prepare to be eaten!"

CHAPTER 21

What? Be eaten? That doesn't sound good! You'd probably like to know more about what happened there, right? Well, you're just going to have to wait, because at the moment, Lilo was pretty busy with her own problems.

"Perhaps you haven't heard, so I'll explain. My name is Zoolox the Unreasonable?" the Snailien said. "Meaning I'm not very reasonable?"

"But why?" Lilo asked.

"Why? Why am I unreasonable?" Zoolox said. "I . . . I don't know. I guess maybe it has to do with my childhood. . . ."

While Lilo kept Zoolox talking, Jumba and Pleakley made their way to the IMDARB and took on the task of disarming the device.

"Do you have any idea how to stop this thing?" Pleakley asked.

"Sure, many ideas," Jumba said. "Most of them involve hitting it with wrench. Say, do you happen to have wrench on you?"

"Yes," Pleakley said.

"Why do you have wrench?" Jumba asked.

"For sentimental reasons!" Pleakley said. "But you can't just hit that thing with a wrench! That's not going to work! It'll, I don't know, explode or something!"

"Most likely." Jumba shrugged. "So will try it old-fashioned way."

Then Jumba ran his fingers along the side of the IMDARB device. He pressed a button, and a panel popped off, revealing a mass of circuitry and wires.

"Cut the red wire! The red one!" Pleakley shouted.

"There is no red wire," Jumba pointed out.

"Sorry. I just always wanted to say that," Pleakley said.

It was at this point that Zoolox realized exactly what was going on.

"Hey! You were just making me talk so I would forget about the IMDARB!" Zoolox said to Lilo before turning on the other two aliens. "What are you bozos doing? Get away, bozos!" Zoolox started to slide back toward the IMDARB.

Suddenly, Lilo jumped right on top of Zoolox and punched him in his big, squishy head.

"Hey! Stop that!" Zoolox shouted.

"You stay away from my friends!" Lilo said.

"Look, that hurts," the Snailien said as he

shuffled around, trying to throw Lilo off. But she hung on tight and kept on punching.

"Now would be a good time to deactivate that thing," Lilo shouted.

"You can't rush genius," Jumba said, studying the insides of the machine.

"Have I ever told you the story of the time I ate a tiny blue alien who was the biggest nuisance in the known galaxies?"

Stitch dove out of the way as the enormous Snailien lunged at him. The creature's mouth just missed swallowing Stitch whole.

"Stitch not hear that one," the alien said.

"It's a doozy," the Snailien replied. "Oh, but where are my manners? My name is Flootbar. Flootbar the Invincible! Now do me a favor and let me devour you."

But Stitch wasn't in the mood to do any favors, so he kept on running, zigzagging and crisscrossing the metal beams. Try as he might, Flootbar couldn't even come close to catching Stitch.

"Say, are you going to stay still so I can eat you or not?" Flootbar asked. "I mean, I'm starting to take this personally!"

"Stitch have better idea," the alien said. He remembered what Jumba had said about their encounter with Flootbar. . . .

Snailien talked. So much talk. Too much talk. Long, boring stories. Was like listening to Pleakley.

I still resent that!

This gave Stitch an idea. He suddenly stopped running and sat down right in front of Flootbar. "Tell Stitch story, please."

Flootbar had opened his mouth, ready to swallow up Stitch, when he said, "Wait. You . . . you actually *want* to hear one of my stories?"

Stitch nodded.

"No one has *ever* wanted to listen to my stories before," Flootbar said, tearing up. "Why, this might be the happiest day of my life!"

And Flootbar proceeded to tell Stitch about the time he watched paint dry on the biggest wall in the known galaxies.

From that moment on, Stitch had a new friend.

"Zoolox, look who I met!" Flootbar said as he oozed onto the top deck of the Eiffel Tower. Stitch was riding on his head, smiling and waving at Lilo, Pleakley, and Jumba.

"Flootbar?" Zoolox said. "You are the fiercest warrior in the known galaxies! And you have been tamed by a rookie detective?"

"He's my friend, Zoolox," Flootbar said. "Which is more than I can say for you! You order me around and make me eat people. I don't want to eat people! Sorry, people." Flootbar gave Jumba and Pleakley a sheepish look.

"Apology accepted," Jumba said. "Also, machine is deactivated now." He held up a handful of wires. "Didn't know which one to cut, so cut them all."

"You cut them all?" Zoolox shouted. "You fool, you've doomed everyone!"

"Really?" Lilo asked.

"No," Zoolox said. "That's pretty much how you stop it."

"Then I guess that's the end of your evil Snailien plan, Zoolox," Lilo said.

"It would appear so," Zoolox said. "For now!"

Then he spat a staggering amount of Snail Slime at Stitch, Lilo, Jumba, Pleakley, and Flootbar!

It all happened so quickly that no one had time to avoid it. Stitch thought for sure that the slime would melt them all. But to his surprise, the slime formed a giant bubble around them. . . .

CHAPTER 22

By the time Stitch managed to tear through the large slime bubble, Zoolox had already disappeared without a trace.

"Where do you think he'll go?" Lilo asked the group.

"Back to Gastropodia, maybe," Flootbar said with a shrug. "Or perhaps he'll stay here on Earth and hide away so he can make more trouble later. But if that happens, I will be here to help you, friends."

"Thanks, Flootbar," Stitch said, and gave him a pat on the side.

With the Snailiens defeated, Stitch quickly ran around the Eiffel Tower, pulling down the wires that had connected the IMDARB to the structure. Jumba picked up the IMDARB itself and hoisted it onto his broad shoulders, then carried it down the stairs to the esplanade below.

When the group finally made it to the ground, the crowd that had gathered around to see the commotion let out a loud cheer.

"They're cheering for you, Stitch!" Lilo said with a proud grin.

Stitch smiled and looked at Lilo. "For all of us!" he replied.

They walked back to the RV. Lilo climbed inside, followed by Jumba and Pleakley.

"I guess this is where we say goodbye," Flootbar said, frowning.

"Why don't you come with us?" Stitch asked.

Flootbar shook his head. "Now that Zoolox is gone, I can finally pursue my true passion!"

"Goodbye, my friends," Flootbar said, waving them off as Stitch entered the RV.

Stitch settled in the driver's seat and took out the galactic communicator. A moment later, the hologram of the Grand Councilwoman appeared.

"Case solved!" Stitch said proudly.

"Remarkable work, Agent 626!" the Grand Councilwoman said enthusiastically. "You and your friends have solved the mystery and prevented the evil Snailiens from invading Earth. The GDA informs me that the Snailiens are in full retreat. We're no longer picking up their signals. Of course, Zoolox is still out there somewhere, but I believe that's a job that Captain Gantu can handle. Possibly."

Hey!
I heard that!

"But I am afraid we do not have much time to celebrate," the Grand Councilwoman said. "Because the GDA needs your help. There is . . . a mystery that requires your attention, in a place I believe you call New York City."

"What kind of mystery?" Stitch asked.

"An *alien* mystery," Agent Bubbles said as he appeared next to the Grand Councilwoman. "We believe that Zoolox had help constructing his IMDARB device. That's what I was investigating before I was captured. We also believe that whoever helped him is still on Earth, seeking to cause untold chaos."

"Agent Bubbles will meet you in New York and help you however he can," the Grand Councilwoman added. "But we will need all your detection skills, Agent 626. Are you up for the challenge?"

Stitch grinned. "Agent 626, ready for duty!" he said as the call disconnected.

"Wait!" Pleakley exclaimed, rounding on Stitch. "We can't just go to New York!"

"Why not?" asked Jumba.

"Because what am I going to tell—" Pleakley started, but the sound of a phone ringing stopped him. He pulled out his galactic communicator. "Nani!"

"Answer it," said Lilo.

"I can't," Pleakley said. "She thinks we just took a field trip in Hawai'i! She doesn't know we even *went* to Paris, let alone that we're planning on going to New York City!"

"Hmmm . . ." Stitch said. "Stitch have idea. Tell the truth!"

"Tell the truth?" Pleakley said, beside himself. "Are you out of your mind?"

Finally, Pleakley picked up the call.

"Pleakley!" Nani said. "Where are you? I thought you'd be home from the field trip by now. What is happening? Is everything okay?"

For a moment, Pleakley said nothing. In fact, he just stared, looking like this:

"Everything is great!" he answered quickly. Then he babbled, "We-were-having-so-much-fun-with-the-Biggest-Ball-of-Twine-and-we-lost-track-of-time-so-we're-camping-out-tonight-and-maybe-tomorrow-night-too-but-we'll-call-you-soon-okay-thanks-bye!"

He hung up.

"Yes, that will work better than the truth," Jumba said.

As the RV rocketed away from the Eiffel Tower, Stitch laughed loudly and shouted, "Next stop, the Big Apple!"

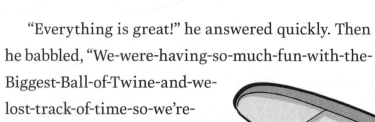

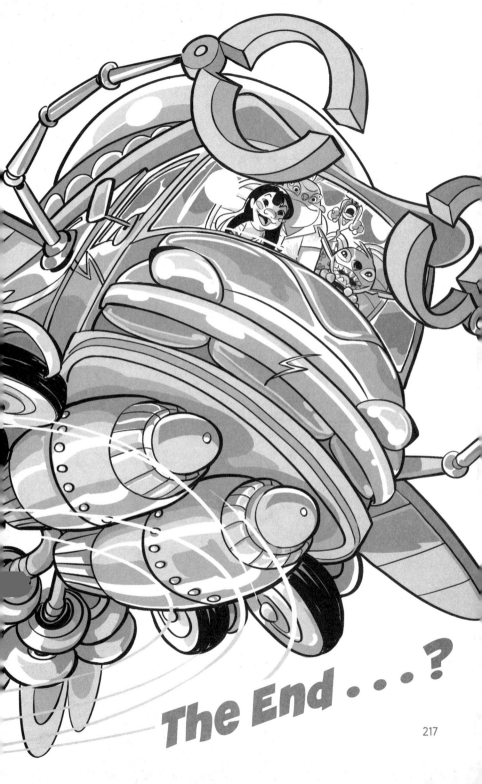

The End . . . ?

217

AUTHOR ACKNOWLEDGMENTS

Simply put, writing this book has been a dream.
I love *Lilo & Stitch*—it's one of my all-time favorite
films. I love the characters (wish I was Stitch, but
I'm definitely Pleakley). So I can't thank my editor,
Holly P. Rice, enough. Without Holly's creativity and
enthusiastic editorial vision, this book wouldn't
exist. I'd also like to thank Elana Cohen, who
suggested me for this project in the first place.
Last, an enormous thank-you to my wife, Nina, who
might just love *Lilo & Stitch* more than I do. Now
if you'll excuse me, I'm off to deliver this peanut-
butter sandwich to Pudge.

ABOUT THE AUTHOR

Steve Behling would take the red ship, likes Elvis, and sinks in water, but swears he is not an alien. Regardless, he's written the completely bonkers junior novel adaptation of *Dora and the Lost City of Gold* and the original middle-grade novels *Avengers Endgame: The Pirate Angel, the Talking Tree, and Captain Rabbit* and *Onward: The Rise of the Phoenix Gem*, to name a few. Steve lives in a top-secret subterranean lair with his wife, two human children, and three-legged wonder beagle Loomis.

ABOUT THE ILLUSTRATOR

Arianna Rea is an artist based in Rome, Italy.
She has been working for the past fifteen years
as a comic book artist, illustrator, and character
designer for the Italian and international markets,
collaborating with big companies such as Disney,
Toei Animation, Egmont, Glénat, Soleil, and Dupuis.
Among her latest works are the adventures of the
young Disney heroes of Princess Beginnings and
Before the Story.